DREAM OF WRITING

An Original Screenplay

Gregory L. Fischer

DREAM OF WRITING

An Original Screenplay

Make It Write Publishing

Make It Write
Baton Rouge, Louisiana

For B & Pops.

A screenwriter.

Contents

Introduction

It's been over 13 years since I began writing the screenplay you are about to read. That's a dismally long time to write anything in my opinion (without it seeing the light of day). Earlier this year, I read *The Bell Jar* by Sylvia Plath and kind of dug into her a little. She once said, "Nothing stinks like a pile of unpublished writing." I got to thinking, this paper pile has been in my closet for way too long. I need to review it again and share it.

That's what I've done. Over the past several months, I have been dedicated to this work. I was prompted also due to artist and writer Anthony Figaro of *Gods Hand*. In April, I chose to write a screen adaptation of his incredibly fun comic book series dedicated to Jean Lafitte. It loosened me up and got me back into Final Draft and thinking seriously about screenwriting again. Thanks, Tony!

I began writing *The Dream of Writing* (notice I dropped the "The") as an undergraduate at LSU. I concentrated on screenwriting for my degree in creative writing, and I don't regret it even though I haven't sold a script, nor have I ever worked a day on a movie set. It's not necessarily that I didn't want to, but I'm my own worst enemy. I even moved to Los Angeles with a little dream in 2012 in hopes to work on this script and sell it, but it didn't work out like I wanted. A year later I returned home to New Orleans, tail between my legs.

I studied at LSU under Rick Blackwood, without whom I wouldn't be half as interested in movies. His class was by far one of the most memorable and valuable that I took in college, and I still consider him my friend.

I also studied under Mari Kornhauser, a true LSU gem. Mari made the seniors write the first two acts of an original screenplay in order to graduate. Looking back at myself at 26, a college radio deejay and restaurant bartender, it's a wonder sometimes how I ever got through.

Thus, this screenplay was started in Mari's capstone writing class. It was a lot different. I was pushing boundaries with sexuality and drug use in my writing because I was immature. For instance, there was a whole scene where Ramen utterly misbehaves with his imaginary muse, Sheila. Remnants of that stuff remain. But most were cut out and rewrote so that the story could be more in-line with what I have to say as a writer at 40.

Lastly, my cousin Mackie's death this year threw me into a whirlwind. I published a memoir called *The Mayor of Mardi Gras*, a collection of anecdotes and illustrations dedicated to my honorary brother and mentor. It was my sister-in-law who read the memoir, and (although never got to meet Mackie) said she could see him becoming a recurring character in my stories from here on out. Thus, I was inspired to add Mackie to the script as Ramen's cousin and coworker.

When I'm writing a scene that includes Mackie, it makes this art form much less lonely.

Gregory L. Fischer
September 26, 2022

If you've never read a screenplay:

INT. means "interior." It lets the director know that the shot occurs indoors. Likewise, EXT. means "exterior." It lets the director know that the shot occurs outdoors.

INT./EXT. is for scenes that require both indoor and outdoor shooting, like a car ride or maybe from an entranceway to a building or a window.

Particular SHOTS are capitalized. Also, when I CAPITALIZE certain terms in the action paragraphs, I'm signaling either the introduction of a new character or things that need extra attention when shooting the scene, or something that needs to be built or included in a scene.

A MONTAGE is a way to move the plot forward more quickly. It's usually a series of short, punchy scenes perhaps the length of one song and may feature dialogue.

Each scene break requires a basic transition. Several different styles of transitions are used: CUT, FADE, DISSOLVE, MATCH CUT, JUMP CUT, SMASH CUT, etc. I didn't label each transition because a basic cut is often all you need.

INSERT means we are inserting something into the scene such as a photograph, text message, letter, or computer screen.

POV means "point of view." SLO-MO is short for "slow-motion."

INTERCUT means the scene cuts back and forth between two places, typically during a phone call.

O.S. means "off-screen," and V.O. means "voice-over."

A BEAT signifies a sound to cue the audience's attention on something. The beat is either part of the movie's score or any sound relative to the scene.

DREAM OF WRITING

MAIN CHARACTERS
(as they appear)

JUDAS (THE ALLIGATOR MAN)
RANDALL STEVENS
RAMEN NOODLE
JILL LAFON
PROFESSOR GREEN
MELODY
SARA BISHOP
DAVE COOLEY
WOMAN IN RED
SHEILA BROWNSTONE
MOM
JACQUES GAUTREAUX
DOUG MILLS
COUSIN MACKIE
LOUISE
OUNGAN

ON WHITE

INSERT – QUOTE

"Absinthe makes the heart grow fonder." —Miss Quoted

DISSOLVE TO:

DREAM OF WRITING

EXT. RURAL HIGHWAY, LOUISIANA – NIGHT (A DREAM)

An ANTIQUE TRUCK cruises up an empty two-way highway through SUGAR CANE fields.

Appears to be a BODY in the TRUCK BED.

INT./EXT. ANTIQUE TRUCK – NIGHT

"Heebie Jeebies," by Louis Armstrong plays softly on the radio.

The truck is being driven by JUDAS: a walking, talking nightmare of CREOLE descent, 40ish. He shrouds his towering physique with a BLOOD-RED, HOODED ROBE.

SKULL RING

On one of his thick fingers gripping the top of the steering wheel.

PASSENGER SEAT

His MASK, formerly an ALLIGATOR'S HEAD.

Also on the seat, a WOODEN BOX the size of a shoebox. The box con-

tains the EVIL SPIRIT OF OBSESSION. The spirit causes the box to GLOW RED like a lamp. The red light shines through cutouts like a jack-o'-lantern on the box.

The cutouts are in the shape of VOODOO EMBLEMS: a HEART PIERCED BY A DAGGER, an ALLIGATOR, and other veve-style lines and shapes.

ALLIGATOR-SKIN BOOT

Presses the brake pedal.

DIRT ROAD

The truck veers off the highway onto a dirt road and reaches a STEEL GATE. It's locked.

FROM INSIDE THE LOCK

Judas inserts the KEY.

He drives ahead, not worried about locking the gate behind him.

JUDAS'S POV

As he drives on the dirt road toward a FOREST.

JUDAS
(deeply; solo)
I have something to give you, mistress.

The truck reaches the forest and stops. Looks like a TRAILHEAD.

EXT. TRAILHEAD/TRAILWAY – NIGHT

Judas steps out of the truck, wearing the alligator mask.

He opens the TRUCK BED to reveal a lifeless BODY wrapped in a bloody, white linen sheet. The sheet is tied by rope at the ankles and neck.

THUD, as the wrapped body hits the ground.

JUDAS'S POV THROUGH THE MASK

Trudging down the trail with the glowing box under one arm, and dragging the body by the rope that's wrapped around its neck.

SOUNDS of fallen leaves and sticks cracking as they go.

SNAKE – ON THE TRAIL

A beat as it slithers out of the way.

EXT. WORSHIP SITE, FOREST – NIGHT

Judas reaches a clearing in the forest: trees bearing VOODOO-STYLE SYMBOLS; an ALTAR as the centerpiece, decorated with a variety of BONES, CANDLES, a half-drank BOTTLE of rum, PIG and CHICKEN parts, and since Judas bears traits of an alligator, ALLI-GATOR parts.

THE BOX

Resting in front of the altar, glows redder.

CANDLES

LIGHT UP without any human assistance in sync with the glow of the box.

ANIMAL PARTS

With FLIES swarming.

He picks up the body and plops it on the altar.

He uses a DAGGER to cut the ropes and the sheet, revealing the handsome face of a MALE: freshly dead, 19-year-old RANDALL STEVENS, who wears a FOOTBALL JERSEY and was once a quarterback.

Randall's bludgeoned HEAD suggests the story of his murder.

Next, Judas cuts Randall's THROAT and catches some dark BLOOD in his hand, and DRINKS.

He kneels before the altar as LIGHTNING strikes.

RAIN starts to fall, and the Alligator Man laughs, menacingly.

In another streak of lightning, he rises, gazes over the body, and feasts on it, ending the dream.

DISSOLVE TO:

INT. RAMEN'S BEDROOM – DAWN

RAMEN NOODLE (pronounced rā-men, *often goes by "Ray"), 22, handsome, ATHLETIC BUILD, pops up suddenly in his DOUBLE BED from a nightmare.*

He shudders and sighs.

A bright streak of LIGHTNING through the window and a loud burst of THUNDER makes him jump.

A fly buzzes around his head. He swats at it a couple of times before giving up angrily.

> RAMEN
> (quietly)
>
> Damn it!

INSERT – DIGITAL CLOCK

Reads 6:00am.

He doesn't want to get up yet and sighs again.

INSERT – DATE

Friday, April 13, 2007 (in courier font)

He reaches for a stereo REMOTE somewhere in the bed.

A MONTAGE begins as he turns on a CD MIXTAPE to get this day started: JAZZ, "Gloria's Step" by the Bill Evans Trio.

He flips on a LAMP next to his bed.

Welcome to Ramen's studio apartment, comprised of a BEDROOM, a BATHROOM, and a KITCHEN. The FRONT DOOR is in the bedroom next to a long WINDOW, and a short HALLWAY doubling as a closet connects the kitchen.

He has HIGH SCHOOL FOOTBALL TROPHIES, WRITING AWARDS, POSTERS of JACK KEROUAC, THE WHITE STRIPES, BOBBY HEBERT, and NINA SIMONE on the walls.

He digs for a leftover JOINT in an ashtray.

> (to himself)
> What is in this weed?

He lights the joint, takes a drag, and coughs.

He stands up to stretch, wearing boxer shorts.

INT. RAMEN'S BATHROOM

Standing in the little bathroom, Ramen stares at himself blankly, if not bewildered, in the mirror.

He starts the FAUCET and runs water over his stubbly face and through his dark hair.

INT. RAMEN'S KITCHEN – DAY

The sun is up through a WINDOW over the sink. He enters the kitchen shaven and showered, wearing a BLOOD RED bath towel at the waist.

KEURIG

A cup of coffee brews.

HIS POV

Mixing two EGGS with a splash of water, butter, pouring them into a CAST-IRON SKILLET, and adding some diced HAM for an OMELETTE.

He walks away.

BEDROOM

The song changes to the UPBEAT drum snares of "A Night in Tunisia," by Art Blakey & The Jazz Messengers.

Ramen dresses in new cargo shorts and a T-shirt bearing a graphic for the movie E.T. from a laundry pile on the floor.

A beat as the SMOKE ALARM goes off.

He peeks his head down the short hall to see the skillet on FIRE.

RAMEN

    Oh no!

KITCHEN

Ramen extinguishes the fire with a big cup of WATER from the sink. He removes the hot skillet from the burner, burning his hand.

RAMEN

    Shit!

He shakes off the pain with a handful of ICE from the freezer.

He fans the smoke alarm with a towel until it stops.

BURNT OMELETTE

Voilà! The watery mass lands on a plate via SPATULA.

He takes an unsatisfying bite and dumps the rest in a nearby trashcan.

BEDROOM

He puts on socks and shoes.

He picks up his SCHOOLBAG, and he powers off the CD Player. As "A Night in Tunisia" ends, so does the montage.

DISSOLVE TO:

EXT. RAMEN'S APARTMENT – DAY

Ramen unlocks his average-looking BICYCLE at the bike rack.

STUDENTS are coming and going.

A beat when he notices a stunningly-attractive brunette, JILL LAFON, 21, walking by serenely, wearing HEADPHONES, holding SCHOOLBOOKS.

She's listening to "Dark of the Matinee" by Franz Ferdinand.

They make eye-contact, and she smiles in passing.

                    JILL'S VOICE
                     (thinking)
          Hi, handsome!

He smiles back.

                   RAMEN'S VOICE
                     (thinking)
          Never seen you before––

He mounts his bicycle and rolls on ahead of her to ORLEANS UNIVERSITY.

INT. COLLEGE CLASSROOM – DAY

The classroom consists of 20 or so DESKS. Only 10 or 12 seats are ever occupied by Ray's CLASSMATES.

He sits in the back row with his notebook open, twirling a PEN.

They hang on every word of PROFESSOR EDWARD GREEN's screenwriting lecture.

Green, 55, former bodybuilder, tall and fit, commands respect (and gets it) but can be downright intimidating to everyone.

> PROFESSOR GREEN
> What happens after you graduate? Should you go to film school? Or should you walk out and go right now? I might go, if I were you . . . if this is what you want. We've heard that Louisiana is widening the gate for Hollywood, but it ain't quite there yet. Remember, I grew up in Podunk County. After I served, I wasn't back home for two months before thinking, "There has to be more than this."
> *(a beat)*
> Turns out I was right! I drive a great car. Absolutely no debt. Looking back, I realize I could still be somewhere bagging groceries.

Ramen's classmate, SARA BISHOP, blond, 20, makeup way overdone, sighs when Green walks past her in the FRONT ROW.

Ramen sits next to a long-standing colleague in the writing program, MELODY, stoned, pretty, but refuses to shave because of feminism.

> MELODY
> *(whispers)*
> Psst. Ray––

RAMEN
(whispers)
What's up Mel?

She grins like she's up to something.

MELODY
I ran into Green last night in the French Quarter. He was wasted.

Ramen smiles.

(grins)
He said something to the effect of his car equals pussy.

Ramen snorts.

(holding back laughter)
He knows I'm lesbian, but I'm like, "Slow down, dude," you know ... I'm still a woman.

Green flashes a look at them.

PROFESSOR GREEN
What the hell is so funny back there?

RAMEN
Melody farted––

MELODY
No, I didn't!

Some classmates laugh a little. Green's expression goes stern.

PROFESSOR GREEN
(to class)
If anyone feels like I'm wasting their time,

we can go home early.

No one moves.

Professor Green gathers himself.

Sara Bishop looks at Ramen disapprovingly.

Ramen waves at her, then flicks her off when she turns around.

Okay, what were we talking about?

SARA BISHOP
Film school?

PROFESSOR GREEN
Thank you.

RAMEN
(whispers, to Melody)
I might actually hate Sara Bishop.

Melody writes something big in a notebook.

NOTEBOOK
She holds it up for Ramen to read: B–I–S–H.

Ramen laughs.

PROFESSOR GREEN
God, Noodle! Are we in high school?

RAMEN
(embarrassed)
I'm so sorry.

PROFESSOR GREEN
(sighs)
Alright.

> *(moving on)*
> I won't sugarcoat it. It's not about talent. It takes plenty of luck to make it in this business. Is it possible? Yes. Is it likely? No, not really.
> *(a beat)*
> Good luck! That's all for today. Real quick––I have graded scenes for you before you leave!

Ramen and his classmates pile up near the doorway.

Green stands in their way, calling out NAMES as he hands back graded scenes to the students.

> *(one by one)*
> Sally May, there you are. Have a good afternoon. Doug Mills, thanks. Melody, cool stuff! Ah, Ramen Noodle:

Ramen faces Green with Melody by his side. Green hands him a PARTIAL SCRIPT, folded in half.

Ramen opens up the fold, revealing the title: "HEAT INDEX," with an "F" and RED INK all over each page.

RAMEN

An "F"?

PROFESSOR GREEN

Looks like you need some work there. Frankly, I'm not impressed. It's lazy. And it lacks imagination. "Heat Index?"

RAMEN

It's a romance.

PROFESSOR GREEN

I didn't get that, at all.

A beat as they look at one another.

Aren't you a screenwriting major?

> RAMEN

Yes.

> PROFESSOR GREEN

Are you sure? . . . Come by my office if you want help, Ramen.

INT. UNIVERSITY BUILDING HALLWAY – DAY

Ramen exits down the hall with Melody. They hear Green hand out a few more scripts before going inaudible:

> PROFESSOR GREEN

Michael Wynn, thank you. Cade Cooper, alright. Sara Bishop––very good work!

> MELODY

Hey, you're a good writer, Ray. You can get this.

> RAMEN
> (defeated)

I don't know. I spend so much friggin' time at the Shipwreck lately.

> MELODY

You might have to change that, you know? How are your other classes going?

> RAMEN

This screenwriting capstone is all I have left to graduate.

> MELODY

Ugh! Really? I'm so jealous. I have a full

plate. Don't let me down, man. I want to
walk the stage with you next month.

                    RAMEN
Same here.

                    MELODY
I believe in you, buddy!

                    RAMEN
Thanks.

                    MELODY
See you Monday.

                    RAMEN
See you.

They part ways.

INT./EXT. VOODOO GIFT SHOP, FRENCH QUARTER – DAY

Ramen stops his bicycle in front of a DISPLAY WINDOW at a voodoo shop across the street from the Shipwreck.

Shelves display ITEMS like wooden statues, beaded jewelry, and kitschy pin dolls.

He notices a linen shirt embroidered with oddly-familiar VOODOO VEVE symbols.

A beat when he finally eyes a wooden box like the one from his dream. While it's not glowing, it bears something similar.

BOX CARVING
In the shape of a heart pierced with a dagger.

We see the man behind the counter, JACQUES GAUTREAUX, skel-

eton-thin (especially in the FACE), middle-aged, Creole, wearing a black collared SHIRT and helping a customer.

JACQUES' POV

As he notices Ramen outside with his hands and face awkwardly pressed against the display window for a moment before turning his bike in the other direction.

INT. THE SHIPWRECK BAR, FRENCH QUARTER – DAY

The SHIPWRECK is the BARROOM where Ramen works and hangs out. Right now he's taking up a BARSTOOL, mulling over his "F".

The space is RECTANGULAR with a row of BOOTHS, a few TA-BLES, and a MARITIME DECOR: dusty anchors, fake palm trees, wooden ships in bottles; and a JUKEBOX now playing "Helpless," by Crosby, Stills, Nash & Young.

Ramen slouches on the bar behind a half-empty pint of LAGER, a lit CIGARETTE stuck to his bottom lip.

DAVE COOLEY dries off pints behind the bar. Dave is Ramen's co-worker and PAL, 30s, stoic, dressed in UNIFORM: a pressed white shirt rolled up to his elbows bearing TATTOOED FOREARMS, silk vest, black pants, and black shoes.

A curvaceous professional WOMAN in a RED SKIRT SUIT and low-cut blouse sits behind a ROMANCE NOVEL a couple seats away from Ramen, drinking a MARTINI.

Three TOURISTS sit in a booth, softly chatting about sightseeing in New Orleans.

Dave throws the towel over his shoulder as he moves to face Ramen.

DAVE

      Everything going all right there, Noodle?
      You seem low.

                    RAMEN
My life is fucked, Dave. Ashes to ashes.

His long cigarette ASH accidentally falls into his beer.

Dust to dust.

Dave smirks.

He pours Ray a new beer.

                    DAVE
This, too shall pass . . . Aren't you supposed
to be at work in a few hours?

                    RAMEN
Story of my life. Thanks for the beer.

                    DAVE
I'll take it out of your tips at some point . . .
Pace yourself!

                    RAMEN
College is bullshit.

                    DAVE
You're preaching to the choir! As soon as I
realized I could support myself bartending,
I kissed all those professors goodbye.

                    RAMEN
Hero.

                    DAVE
                  (*a beat*)
I'm no hero. Don't you graduate soon?

RAMEN

Ugh. We'll see. I failed this big assignment today.

DAVE

(*lights a cigarette*)

You can pick that up. C'mon, don't be a fool. I would've finished if I was that close . . . What happens after you finish? Let's talk about that.

RAMEN

(*sighs*)

I don't know. I don't know if I'm ready.

DAVE

Ready or not, here it comes.

Ramen lights another cigarette.

The WOMAN IN RED peeks at them over her novel.

Is it gonna be "Mr. Noodle," the English teacher, soon?

RAMEN

Who wants that?

DAVE

I know, Ramen. You're gonna be a big shot Hollywood screenwriter, right?

RAMEN

Actually, I'm thinking about writing your biography. It's called, "The Radical Life of a Nouveau French Quarter Rat."

DAVE
Nouveau? I've been here seven years, buddy
. . . What do you think you are?

The woman puts her romance novel down.

WOMAN IN RED
(interrupting)
Can you write me a new romance novel,
handsome?

She has their attention.

I'm getting tired of reading this junk.

RAMEN
How about a movie?

WOMAN IN RED
I like movies . . .

RAMEN
What do you do for a living, miss? If you
don't mind me asking.

WOMAN IN RED
I'm an attorney.
(to Dave)
You got a pen, barkeep?

Dave pulls a pen from his shirt pocket and hands it to her.

She writes something on a white bar NAPKIN.

DAVE
Another dirty martini?

HER MOUTH

As she bites the olive.

WOMAN IN RED

If I drink another one, I might need a ride home.

DAVE
(shrugs)

Make my day.

WOMAN IN RED

You're sweet. What do I owe you?

He slides her a BILL. She lays a TWENTY on the bar and gets up.

She places the bar napkin in front of Ramen.

INSERT – NAPKIN

With her phone number on it.

RAMEN'S LINE OF SIGHT

Rises from her bosom to meet her gaze.

She winks at him:

(to Ramen)

Call me.

She puts on designer SUNGLASSES and sashays out the door.

DAVE

. . . She loves playing games with me.

RAMEN

What? I just killed it with the sad-puppy routine.

DAVE

Routine? Please, you're the genuine article
. . . You gonna call her? Maybe do the Red
Dress Run together?

RAMEN

Maybe.

Dave grabs for the napkin, but Ramen's faster.

DAVE
(concedes)

Whatever––I'll get it. She's been reading
her romance novels in front of me for three
weeks.

RAMEN
(shrugs)

. . . The script that I failed today was a romance.

Dave laughs.

DAVE

You obviously don't know shit about romance.

RAMEN
(smirks)

Up yours.
(a beat)
Hey, man, you know anything about voodoo?

DAVE

No, but why?

                    RAMEN
I had a nightmare last night.

                    DAVE
Oh, God, don't bore me with your dreams.

                    RAMEN
No, listen! This alligator-man ate this guy on
a voodoo altar. It was scary stuff.

                    DAVE
Alligator Man? Might be time to quit smoking weed.

                    RAMEN
It felt so real.

                    DAVE
I'm failing to connect the voodoo dots.

                    RAMEN
Well, the monster had this strange lamp. It
looked like a shoebox. He carried it every
step of the way and then, like, prayed to it
or something. It had symbols on it that were
glowing red--voodoo symbols.

                    DAVE
I don't know. You ever meet Jacques from
the voodoo shop?

                    RAMEN
The skeleton?

                    DAVE
He's a skinny dude. He comes in after work
sometimes. Kind of quiet, but cool. You

might want to introduce yourself.

"Ready or Not" by The Fugees begins playing on the jukebox, and a MONTAGE begins.

Ramen takes the last sip of his beer.

RAMEN

Thanks, man. I'm going home for a little while.

DAVE

Sure thing. Don't be late tonight. A new bartender's starting.

Ramen picks up his bicycle, which was leaning on a table.

He exits out the door.

EXT. NEW ORLEANS STREETS – DAY

Ramen rides his bike through the New Orleans French Quarter, taking in the sights and sounds to the beats of The Fugees.

He passes street artists, tarot readers, the row of mule drawn carriages in front of the St. Louis Cathedral, a line of people in front of Café Du Monde, the French Market, jazz clubs on Frenchmen St., and Baldwin & Co. Bookstore.

Next, he rides through Gentilly, passing children playing in a schoolyard, St. Augustine High School, Popeye's, Parisite DIY Skatepark, Fair Grounds Race Course, Brother Martin High School, and High School Cross Country runners practicing on the Lake Pontchartrain levee.

Finally, he passes Orleans University and reaches his apartment building.

He LOCKS his bike at the rack.

He steps inside.

INT. RAMEN'S BEDROOM – CONTINUOUS

Ramen drops his backpack by the door.

He kicks off his sandals.

He sits in a PAPASAN CHAIR.

He pulls a nearby ottoman closer. A FULL ASHTRAY rests on top of it.

Ramen puts his feet up on the ottoman anyway, avoiding the ashtray.

He turns on the TV.

He falls asleep, and the montage ends.

INT. CHURCH SACRISTY – NIGHT (A DREAM)

JUDAS, dressed like a priest in a black suit with no mask, folds a BLOODY, white linen SHEET on a countertop. He's standing inside a lavish sacristy, connected to a large, country church.

The sacristy features a FIREPLACE with a FIRE burning. Judas tosses the sheet in and watches it turn to ASHES.

EXT. GRASS FIELD, OUTSIDE CHURCH – NIGHT

The church rests on acres of land, a very wide-open space.

SHEILA BROWNSTONE, the GORGEOUS only child of a prominent New Orleans judge (and although vivid at times, a complete figment of Ramen's dreams and imagination), a new college student, blond and busty, runs through an open field in a summer dress.

She holds hands with Randall Stevens, who's wearing a football letter-

man jacket over a WHITE collared shirt.

> RANDALL
> I can't wait for us to leave for college.

Sheila frowns.

> Don't make that face, Sheila . . . I just mean
> I can't wait to start playing football games at
> that big stadium. You better come see me!

> SHEILA
> I'm afraid you'll find someone else out there.
> New girls will be throwing themselves at
> you . . . I wish you'd just stay in Louisiana.

> RANDALL
> And what, give up my scholarship? Don't
> say that, Sheila. You're everything to me.
> (smiles)
> I'm sure you'll get hit on, too.

They embrace.

> Sheila, I love you. Whatever comes next, we
> do it together.

> SHEILA
> I love you too, Randy. Be still, my heart.

The two stop to make out sweetly under the moon.

They're interrupted by a woman's SCREAM in the distance.

> What was that?

> RANDALL
> I don't know. Let's go see.

Sheila shakes her head.

C'mon, it came from the behind the church.

                                SHEILA
Then let the priest handle it!

                                RANDALL
What if the priest needs our help! You coming?

                                SHEILA
I've got a bad feeling about this.

Randall begins pacing backwards toward his ANTIQUE TRUCK, the same one we saw Judas drive.

                                RANDALL
Fine, stay here.

                                SHEILA
No! Don't leave me!

                                RANDALL
I'll be right back. Don't worry!

He gets in the truck and speeds away toward the church, and the dream ends.

                                                    DISSOLVE TO:

INT. RAMEN'S BEDROOM – AFTERNOON

Ramen awakens softly, and his EYES glance around the room.

He's unknowingly doing his best Al Bundy impersonation, reclining in the papasan chair, feet up, one hand wedged in his shorts.

INSERT – TV

MAURY, the topic: "real paternity tests."

INT. MOM'S HOUSE – DAY

Ramen's MOM, a divorced secretary-type, lives in a modest New Orleans shotgun home, small but decorated well enough. FIFTY-FIVE, HEALTHY, and PETITE, she's in a BATHROBE painting her NAILS at the DINING ROOM TABLE.

CELL PHONE

She picks it up from the table.

INSERT – CONTACTS LIST

She scrolls to "Son."

BACK TO:

RAMEN'S BEDROOM

Ramen's CELL PHONE rings from his DESK to the tune of "Don't Stop Believin'" by Journey. He knows who it is.

He gets up to answer, but he forgot about the full ashtray next to his foot on the ottoman—CRASH!

> RAMEN
>
> Ugh!
> (answers)
> Hey mom.

> MOM'S VOICE
>
> Knock knock.

> RAMEN
>
> Who's there?

> MOM'S VOICE
>
> Jamaica.

                         RAMEN
         Jamaica who?

                       MOM'S VOICE
         Jamaica call to ya mama lately?

He wants to laugh, but can't get it out. He takes a seat at the desk.

         You doing okay?

The ashtray broke over a white, collared work shirt on the floor.

                         RAMEN
                        (winces)
         Literally, or figuratively?

                       MOM'S VOICE
         Literally.

                         RAMEN
         Struggling.

INTERCUT

With mom prepping for a night out: toenails, makeup.

                          MOM
         What's going on?

                         RAMEN
         I spilled something on my work shirt.

                          MOM
                        (sighs)
         Ray, if you hang up your clothes this doesn't
         happen.

                         RAMEN
         I know.

MOM
You've been busy?

RAMEN
Yeah, with screenwriting and work.

MOM
Alright, Mr. Screenwriter! I was talking about you with my friend yesterday. I told her you became interested in writing after the divorce.

RAMEN
Whoa! It's not about you! Or dad!

MOM
I never said that!

RAMEN
It's just something I'm passionate about, okay?

MOM
I know, baby. Talk to your dad lately?

RAMEN
No. We don't talk, mom. He's in the sticks, living that double-wide life.

MOM
He still thinks you should be playing football.
(laughs)
Cracks me up!

Ray smirks.

RAMEN
(angrily)
Oh, well, you know! . . . I want to be a writer.

MOM
(soothing)
I'm not trying to upset you. And you will become a writer, Ray. Things take time. Tell me something about screenwriting.

RAMEN
(sighs)
My capstone class is hard. My professor gave me an "F" on this big sequence I had to turn in.

MOM
An "F?" Something's wrong. You're not an "F" student, kiddo.

RAMEN
I don't know. Maybe I am. Maybe I should go full-time at The Shipwreck––

MOM
Full time at the bar?
(scoffs)
Great. You want to be around a bunch of alcoholics your whole life? Suit yourself.

RAMEN
It's just that writing movies is tougher than I thought. It's technical. A lot of detail . . . He said I lack imagination.

MOM
If there's one thing you've got, it's imagination, Ray! Don't let anyone sell you short.

RAMEN
I won't graduate if I don't pass this class.

MOM
(a beat)
Son, remember when you were a kid? What
was your favorite toy?

He notices a bit of a joint on the FLOOR and picks it up.

RAMEN
Toy? I remember dad yelling at me on the
football field:
(imitating his father, the angry coach)
"You won't amount to squat, Ray, if you don't
score a touchdown right here!"

MOM
No, son. I'm not talking about football––
LEGO's. I used to tell people you were going
to be an architect.

Ramen smirks.

You remember building that Robin Hood
castle-thing . . . it was a Christmas present!

RAMEN
(smiles)
I remember it being extremely difficult. I
needed help with the drawbridge.

MOM
All I did was tie a little knot for you. You did
all the hard work.

RAMEN
Mom, what's the point?

MOM

The point is that you're good at putting things together. Even when you were a tiny kid, you loved building blocks. I remember you lugging that heavy crate of wooden blocks into the living room. Piece by piece, I watched you figure out how to build houses and forts. Maybe it's the same with screenwriting, Ray. Write one scene at a time. Like a little building block. Let it all come together, and before you know it, you've written a movie.

RAMEN
(assuaged)

I see what you mean.

MOM

Good! You've got to graduate, son. I know you want to have fun, working in the damn French Quarter . . . But you've got to take time out to write. For you.

He lights the joint.

By the way, my friend said she knows a producer in town who's looking for local movie scripts.

RAMEN
(excitedly)

Really?

MOM

Really! Got any ideas?

He takes a HEAVY drag . . .

EXT. WORSHIP SITE – NIGHT (DREAM FLASHBACK)

An eerie return to the earlier scene of the alligator man FEEDING on the body of Randall.

The box GLOWS brightly.

BACK TO:

RAMEN'S BEDROOM

Ramen's still sitting at his desk on the phone with Mom. He shudders, exhales smoke.

A FLY buzzes around him.

He takes a swat and misses.

INTERCUT

Mom still prepping, brushes her hair.

> MOM
>
> Did I lose you?

> RAMEN
>
> No, sorry. I'm here. I think I'm gonna write a voodoo horror movie.

> MOM
>
> Voodoo?

> RAMEN
>
> "The Alligator Man."

Mom laughs.

> MOM
>
> Alligator Man? What's it about?

RAMEN

An evil alligator monster, eating people, ter-
rorizing a bayou town. I've been thinking
about it today.

MOM

Alligators are scary! But, it sounds like a
classic horror movie to me!

RAMEN

You think?

MOM

I mean, you might need to flesh it out. But
I think you can do it! All those writing
awards––

*We see three PLAQUES from the 10th, 11th, and 12th grade: writing
AWARDS hanging on his bedroom wall read, "Creative Quill Honors,
1st Place—Girard H.S."*

Do you still have those?

RAMEN

They're hanging on my wall.

MOM

It's a good reminder! ––I'll tell my friend
that you're writing a voodoo horror with
a monster. You're gonna have to figure out
the rest. Now shake it off and get to work, or
you'll regret it.

RAMEN

I know. Thanks, mom. I gotta go.

MOM

Love you, Ray!

                    RAMEN
Love you, too.

INT. THE SHIPWRECK BAR – EVENING

A mixed group of patrons populate the bar area. Ramen stands behind the bar SHAKING a drink for someone.

He serves the drink.

Dave's shift has ended, and now he's seated at the bar.

Ray pours Dave a draft beer.

                    DAVE
                (lights a cig)
I've got a new nickname for you––Ramen Krueger!

                    RAMEN
Not funny!

Dave gives him a look:

                    DAVE
Let's see. No noticeable scars. Guess the Alligator Man hasn't returned. Did you cry in a corner all afternoon?

                    RAMEN
I had another dream!

                    DAVE
No way!

                    RAMEN
It was shorter. It wasn't really scary. But it was the same characters. This time the foot-

ball player was alive though. Or maybe he
was gonna die . . .

DAVE
You might need a shrink, Noodle.

RAMEN
(shrugs)
. . . I talked to my mom for a little bit, too.

DAVE
In your dream?

RAMEN
No, in real life.

DAVE
Give her my regards?

RAMEN
(ignores it)
When's the new bartender getting here? We
might be a little busy.

DAVE
Should be here any minute . . .

*A CUSTOMER at the jukebox plays "Strange Desire," by The Black
Keys. The VOLUME is UP.*

*SUDDENLY, the bar door swings open. It's JILL LAFON, who walked
past Ramen this morning.*

SLOW MOTION

*Jill takes a few steps toward Ray, essentially. She's dressed provoca-
tively in a white blouse with black suspenders, a short, black pleated
skirt, black knee-highs and holds a small PURSE.*

JILL'S POV – SLOW MOTION

As she walks in front of the jukebox around the bar: Ramen pours a beer but starts to miss the glass after noticing her. Dave sees her, but he's unaffected and turns back to the bar to notice Ramen's misfire. He reaches over the bar to help Ramen shut off the tap. He's met with a little resistance from Ramen, who's smitten and obviously doesn't realize what he's doing.

As Ramen acquiesces his mistake to Dave, Jill crouches beneath the bar gate to end the slo-mo sequence.

> RAMEN
> My bad! Thanks, man!

Dave, a true friend, doesn't want to embarrass Ramen in front of Jill any further.

> DAVE
> (diverting)
> The music is kinda loud!

Ramen turns down the volume on the jukebox to a soft level with a remote.

> JILL
> Hi. I'm not late, am I?

> RAMEN
> No.

Ramen awkwardly holds out a hand to greet her.

> Ray, nice to meet you.

> JILL
> Jill Lafon.

They shake hands.

                    RAMEN
This is David Cooley.

                    DAVE
                  (waves)
Dave.

                    JILL
Nice to meet you guys!
               (to Ramen)
Is there somewhere I can put my purse?

                    RAMEN
             (points to a spot)
Right here's safe.

Dave GULPS the rest of his beer down.

                    DAVE
Well, I'm leaving. I have a bottle of absinthe
at home waiting for me.

                    JILL
               (to Dave)
Ah, the good stuff!

                    RAMEN
I still gotta try that. What's it like?

                    DAVE
Like dreaming while you're awake.

He winks at Ramen.

                    JILL
               (to Ramen)
I'm surprised you haven't tried it yet, bartender.

Ramen shrugs.

> DAVE
>
> He's not a real bartender.

> JILL
>
> No?

> RAMEN
>
> Don't listen to him.

> DAVE
>
> You'll see. Ramen's a famous writer, biding his time.

> JILL
> *(smiles)*
>
> That's cool I guess.

Dave stands up.

> DAVE
>
> You kids have fun––

> RAMEN
>
> Later, pops!

> JILL
>
> Bye Dave.

> DAVE
> *(upon exit)*
>
> Adios!

> RAMEN
>
> I think I saw you this morning on my way to school.

                    JILL'S VOICE
                     (thinking)
Play it cool.

                       JILL
                    (grimaces)
Sorry. I've seen so many new faces this week.
I just transferred.

                  RAMEN'S VOICE
                     (thinking)
She smiles at everyone.

                      RAMEN
Oh. From where?

                       JILL
Georgetown. I was a premed, but I hated
it. I decided that I didn't want to live in my
mother's shadow my whole life.

                      RAMEN
Bet she loves that.

                       JILL
We had a big talk not too long ago. ——It's
progress, not perfection.

                      RAMEN
Are you from D.C.?

                       JILL
New York City, actually. Manhattan. Pretty
close to NYU. Are you familiar?

                      RAMEN
Never been. But sometimes I feel like I

should be in New York, or Los Angeles.

JILL
Why, what are you studying?

RAMEN
Screenwriting.
(smiles)
With a name like Lafon, I might have pegged
you for a French Louisiana gal.

JILL
I'm not that lucky. I figured New Orleans
would be a great place to study French
though.

*A MALE and a FEMALE TOURIST, retirement age, wearing TROP-
ICAL SHIRTS, approach the bar and sit. The man sets his CAMERA
BAG down.*

MALE TOURIST
(to wife)
Woo, my dogs are barking!

FEMALE TOURIST
It's nice and cool in here, at least.

Jill greets them with a WAVE before she approaches.

JILL
What can I do for you?

MALE TOURIST
(to Jill)
Two Heinekens, please.

She reaches for two Heineys in the cooler.

                    RAMEN
              (smiles; to Jill)
      First two customers!

Jill serves them, then returns.

                    JILL
      Nothing to it. ––So, screenwriting, really? I
      love movies!

                    RAMEN
      Yeah? What's your favorite?

                    JILL
      Oh, man, tough one! Let's see, I like all the
      Stanley Kubrick movies.

                RAMEN'S VOICE
                 (thinking)
      Bonus!

                    JILL
      I like Richard Linklater, Tim Burton, Spike
      Lee, I mean––

                    RAMEN
      You do love movies!

Jill shrugs and smiles.

She throws a BAR TOWEL over her shoulder.

                    JILL
      Okay, my turn! What's your favorite?

                    RAMEN
      Oh, God. I'm kinda into Fellini lately. "8 1/2"

is really interesting.

JILL

Haven't seen it.

RAMEN

It's great. It's about a writer who's stuck inside his head all the time. Can't tell a dream from reality. They say it's autobiographical.

JILL

That sounds cool. Can I ask you a question?

He nods.

(a beat)

I was told I was to be working with Noodle tonight, but Ramen Noodle––Is that your name?

RAMEN

Just like the Japanese pasta. Salt of the earth.

Jill laughs.

JILL

You're not Japanese.

RAMEN

I know!

JILL

That's the funniest thing I've ever heard. Was it even on the market back then?

RAMEN
(shrugs)

I think so.

JILL
Oh my God, I love it!

JACQUES enters the bar, wearing a black FEDORA with a SNAKE-SKIN band and a RED feather. He just closed the voodoo shop for the night. Jill takes notice.

(to Ramen)
This is a great place for character study, huh?

RAMEN
The best!

Jacques sits at the bar. He stands out to the tourists, who can't help but notice him.

JILL
(to Ramen)
Your turn.

RAMEN
(to Jacques)
Hey, how's it going?

JACQUES
(grins)
I suppose it's going well.

RAMEN
Jacques, right?

JACQUES
(to himself)
He knows my name.
(to Ramen)
Yes, and your name?

RAMEN
I'm Ramen. What's your poison?

JACQUES
Dark rum, please. With a splash of Coke.

RAMEN
You got it!

JILL
(to Ramen)
I have to run to the ladies' room.

She walks off. Ray serves Jacques the drink.

JACQUES
Thank you.

RAMEN
How long have you worked at the voodoo shop?

JACQUES
(smiles)
It's my shop. Why, do you like voodoo?

RAMEN
I don't know much about it.

JACQUES
Ever heard of Marie Laveau?

RAMEN
The Voodoo Queen of New Orleeens? Sure.

JACQUES
She was a friend of my family's, back then.

She's still a friend to me . . . You know what I mean?

RAMEN
What, like in spirit?

JACQUES
Exactly. Her spirit.

RAMEN
Can I ask you about something?

JACQUES
Please!

RAMEN
I had a serious nightmare last night, and I think it had something to do with voodoo.

JACQUES
Why voodoo?

RAMEN
Well . . . This guy looked like an alligator. He wore an alligator head. Does that sound like voodoo?

JACQUES
(baffled)
An *alligator* head?

RAMEN
Yeah, like this guy was more of an alligator than a man. It was so real. Plus, he had this box like the one in your shop window. But only it glowed red and had some of those symbols on it. Can you make sense of that? I

can't make any.

                    JACQUES
Sounds . . . scary.

Jill returns behind the bar. She overhears them:

                    RAMEN
It was!

                    JACQUES
Sometimes people make lamps out of ordi-
nary things for voodoo. They add their own
ingredients, such as oils to burn, and it gives
the lamp a unique power. I have to admit,
though, I've never seen one glow red––on its
own.

                    RAMEN
Does voodoo ever involve cannibalism?

Jill gives Ramen a look like he's lost his mind.

The jukebox starts to play "Mother-in-Law" by Ernie K-Doe.

                  MALE TOURIST
                    (to Jill)
Miss, we'd like one more round please, and
then close out.

                     JILL
Right away!

She serves the couple.

                    JACQUES
                   (to Ramen)
In my voodoo, cannibalism would be very bad.

RAMEN

I would hope so.

After a moment they laugh.

JACQUES

Ramen, have you ever been to a voodoo ritual?

RAMEN

No. Do you attend *voodoo rituals?*

JACQUES

Of course! Maybe you would like to come see for yourself?

RAMEN
(grimaces)

I don't know.

JACQUES
(a beat)

In voodoo, we interact with spirits of our ancestors and different deities like they are still a part of our home. Like they live with us. Like a father or even a--mother-in-law.

Ramen smiles.

They often communicate with us through dreams.

RAMEN

Wouldn't I stick out like a sore thumb at a voodoo ritual?

JACQUES

Because you are white?

Ramen nods.

> You might be surprised. If voodoo is what you seek, you're always welcome.

> RAMEN
> I'm failing this big class I need to pass to graduate college. Is there like a spell for that?

> JACQUES
> No. Voodoo is more about communication. Not spells. Perspective is everything . . . Graduation may be the least of your worries.

Jacques finishes his drink.

He leaves some money on the bar.

> RAMEN
> When's the next ritual?

> JACQUES
> Very soon. I can notify you.

> RAMEN
> Would you?

> JACQUES
> I will. Have a good night.

> RAMEN
> You too.

Jacques exits the bar.

EXT. THE SHIPWRECK BAR – LATER THAT NIGHT

Jill and Ramen exit the Shipwreck together. Their shift has ended.

We don't see the late-night bartender, Corinne, but Ramen says good-bye as they leave:

RAMEN
See you Corinne! Have a good shift!

CORINNE'S VOICE
'Night, man! Nice meeting you, Jill!

JILL
(happily)
You too, Corinne!

The door closes, and they are standing in the middle of a BUSTLING French Quarter.

JAZZ MUSIC plays from a club in the distance.

RANDOM PEOPLE walk past them on the street: TOURISTS holding obnoxious-looking drinks and wearing MARDI GRAS BEADS, DRAG QUEENS, and someone in a BATMAN COSTUME.

A YOUNG WOMAN on a BALCONY points to a TOURIST wearing large Carnival beads.

YOUNG WOMAN
Hey, guy, I want those beads!

BEAD GUY
You must think these grow on trees!

BALCONY
Jill and Ramen watch for a minute as she flashes him.

He throws her the beads.

Ramen smirks.

JILL
(to Ramen)
That's the first time I've seen that!

RAMEN
It won't be the last.

JILL
Well . . . That was pretty good for my first
night!

RAMEN
Work, you mean?

JILL
Yeah.

RAMEN
Yeah, nothing too crazy.

He lights a SMOKE and offers Jill one.

JILL
No, thanks. That's bad news.

RAMEN
Hm. Would you like to maybe go have a
drink with me? I know a cool place.

JILL
I would. But I have to meet with a study
group in the morning . . . It's gonna be hard
being a student here.

RAMEN
One day you'll wear it like a badge is what
they say. How about food? I know a spot

where we can get some late night pho.

                    JILL
Miam, miam! I love pho! But I'm not
hungry.

Jill focuses her attention across the street at the VOODOO SHOP.

                 (entranced)
Is that a voodoo shop?

Ramen looks. The voodoo shop is CLOSED.

SHOP WINDOW

A beat as he sees the ALLIGATOR MAN staring at him.

He shudders.

RAMEN'S POV

*When he looks again, he only sees the voodoo ITEMS in the window
for sale.*

                 (to Ramen)
You look like you're thinking. Do you think
a lot?

                   RAMEN
Sorry, I just had the chills. I had a wicked
dream last night. It was about voodoo.

                    JILL
Intriguing. Who was that skinny guy earlier
at the bar?

                   RAMEN
Jacques. He owns this shop.

JILL

Oh. You were having some weird conversation!

RAMEN

Kinda ... Hey, do you need a ride home? I
live in the campus apartments.

JILL

I do too!

RAMEN

I knew I saw you this morning!

JILL

Maybe you did.
                    (smiles)
I was gonna take a cab, but sure!

INT./EXT. JEEP RIDE – NIGHT

*Dr. John's version of "I Walk on Guilded Splinters" plays softly on the
radio of Ramen's OLD JEEP.*

*They're getting to know each other, while driving through the French
Quarter and MARIGNY neighborhoods on their way back home
toward the LAKEFRONT near the university.*

RAMEN

Do you like the neighborhood?

JILL

I can see Lake Pontchartrain over the levee
from my window. It's pretty.

RAMEN

Big lake, huh! I'm on the first floor, opposite
the lake. All I can see are ruins of flooded

houses. Can we trade?

JILL

No. Were you here for Katrina?

RAMEN

Yeah . . . But I transferred to Baton Rouge
for a semester until the city reopened.

JILL

What about your family? Were they okay?

RAMEN

They were okay . . . My parents divorced
when I was in middle school.

JILL

I'm sorry. Mine are still together, but sometimes I wonder how.

RAMEN

Sticking it out, good stuff . . . My apartment
flooded like three feet. I lost all my furniture, a guitar, some video games. My dad's
house flooded. Just about all my aunts' and
uncles'. My mom had some roof damage.

JILL

That's awful.

RAMEN

Yeah, it's been almost two years. Things are
slowly getting back to normal. You're kind
of brave for moving here.

JILL

I wanted to see something different, that's

all. It's an interesting place to be right now.
I'll say that.

RAMEN
One of a kind. Always has been.

They arrive at the campus apartments.

EXT. JILL'S APARTMENT – NIGHT

Ramen walks Jill to her door.

RAMEN
It was fun working with you tonight, Jill.

RAMEN'S VOICE
(thinking)
You're even prettier in the moonlight.

JILL
Nice working with you, too, Ramen Noodle,
the screenwriter.
(beat)
So, what, are you like going to burn the
midnight oil and write tonight?

RAMEN
(shrugs)
I'm kind of tired, but––

JILL
Write something.

Ramen steps back a few feet, then:

RAMEN
(shyly)
Do you want to maybe hang out sometime?

Drink some whiskey, or something?

JILL
How about absinthe?

RAMEN
(smiles)
Absinthe it is! Good night!

JILL
Thanks for the ride.

INT. RAMEN'S BEDROOM – NIGHT

Ramen enters his apartment and turns on a lamp.

He falls backwards on his bed.

RAMEN
(sighs)
What a day!

He turns on the CD player with a REMOTE, and "Show Some Emotion" by Joan Armatrading plays softly.

After a moment he moves to his desk and opens the LAPTOP.

INSERT – COMPUTER SCREEN
He pulls up the SCRIPT we saw earlier, titled "Heat Index."

Next to the laptop, the graded paper with the "F" sits on the desk.

COMPUTER SCREEN
He deletes the script and stares at an empty page.

INSERT – DIGITAL CLOCK
Reads 1:07am.

He looks once more at the failing grade on his script.

Screw this.

He crumples it up.

WASTEBASKET
Swish!

INSERT – COMPUTER SCREEN
He TYPES the first SLUG LINE of his new script:

"EXT. TRAILHEAD - NIGHT
A massive Creole man in a RED robe wearing an ALLIGATOR
HEAD that MASKS his face, steps out of an ANTIQUE TRUCK.

"He's holding a BOX, GLOWING RED underneath one arm and
dragging a DEAD FOOTBALL PLAYER with the other . . ."

FADE TO BLACK:

INT. COLLEGE CLASSROOM – DAY

Ramen sits in class, leaning his head back against the wall. He has an
awful case of BED HEAD.

PROFESSOR GREEN
Can anyone tell me how most screenplays
are read by producers?

INSERT – DATE
Monday, April 16, 2007

CLASSMATE
Uh, left to right?

Some of the students laugh.

PROFESSOR GREEN
Is that a joke?

The CLASSMATE slinks down in their chair.

No. They're gonna read five lines. And do you know what happens to all of your hours—your days, months, years—all that work, all your hopes and dreams . . . If no one gets excited reading the first five lines—it's going in the trash, folks.

MELODY
(to Ramen; whispers)
You look kind of rough.

RAMEN
(whispers back)
I wrote a lot this weekend. I'm drained.

Melody signals a GOLF CLAP to Ray.

Thanks.

PROFESSOR GREEN
(to class)
What, you don't believe me? Here's a story.

RAMEN
(mimicking Green; to Melody)
"Here's a story."

She smiles.

PROFESSOR GREEN
After I sold my first script in Hollywood, for six figures . . . I was invited to a party . . . Ev-

eryone looked real pretty. Models and film execs were drinking expensive liquor, snorting cocaine out in the open––

Sara Bishop raises her hand.

Sara?

SARA BISHOP
Are drugs everywhere in Hollywood?

Green nods.

PROFESSOR GREEN
Sara, the first thing you'll learn in Hollywood is that everyone has a lawyer, a shrink, and a drug dealer.

Some students laugh.

Not kidding! . . . At least back in those days . . . So, I'm at this party in somebody's high-rise condo, mingling, when all of a sudden this guy who's been sitting on a sofa in front of one of these giant projector screens yells out––
(loudly)
"Bad fucking call!"

Most of the class jumps, including Ramen.

Green smirks.

Most people at the party jumped too, like "what on earth?" But get this . . .

He measures from the floor to his waist with a hand.

The guy had a stack of screenplays next to him this high.

SARA BISHOP

Rude.

PROFESSOR GREEN

Rude?

SARA BISHOP

Well, yeah! I mean it sounds like there could've been writers at the party watching him, you know?
(shrugs)
You were there.

PROFESSOR GREEN

I was! And no, he did not care. Not one iota.
(sighs)
Let me just say this: Power does not care about your feelings, okay? . . . This guy was working for one of the major studios. I won't mention any names, but he was reviewing a stack of screenplays in the middle of this party during a freaking Raiders playoff game . . . Now, I'm watching him . . . And I swear to God he was reading less than half of the first page of some of these scripts, and then tossing them back over his shoulder into a pile on the floor.
(smirks)
You still want to be a screenwriter?

The class looks deflated: FROWNING, CONFUSED FACES.

Oh, come on! You guys look like we just got dumped on prom night . . . Cheer up! The message is that this business isn't about how good you are. Sometimes it's just about dumb luck. That's all I'm gonna say about it. Fortunately there are ways to better your chances at being noticed, such as?

DOUG MILLS raises his hand.

Doug.

DOUG
Such as attending a well-known film school?

PROFESSOR GREEN
Good! Name some reputable programs.

DOUG
Doesn't USC have a good film program?

PROFESSOR GREEN
S-C's not bad, Sam Peckinpah came from there. But it looks like a high school with ashtrays.

Students laugh.

You laugh, but it's true … UT-Austin is good. NYU is good. But, I'm a UCLA guy. Can anyone tell me what separates UCLA from other schools?

No one answers.

No one? Okay . . . See, at UCLA, you'll make friends with the most unusual people. They're unusual because they are the daughters and nephews of billionaire film executives . . . That is what makes UCLA—— worthwhile.

Ramen raises his hand.

Ray?

RAMEN
Why is that worthwhile?

PROFESSOR GREEN
Really? It's called power, Ramen. These people . . . they don't play by the same rules as guys like us . . . At UCLA, they'll become your drinking buddies. See what I mean?

Ramen nods.

Good. After all, each one of you is going to need *what* to make your movies, gang?

MELODY
Money.

PROFESSOR GREEN
Correct! A lot of freaking money. They have it over there. You just have to go get it . . . That'll do it for today. Have a great afternoon. Keep going with those revisions! I mean it!

RAMEN'S NOTEBOOK
Bears an empty page.

He puts it away and files out of the classroom.

INT. THE SHIPWRECK BAR, FRENCH QUARTER – NIGHT
Ray and Dave work at the bar together, but it's slow. "Night Rally" by

Elvis Costello & The Attractions plays on the jukebox.

Dave READS MOBY-DICK while standing behind the bar.

Ramen cleans a STACK of PINT GLASSES in the SINK and sets them aside to dry.

Two MIDDLE-AGED MEN, random CUSTOMERS, talk at the far end of the bar.

> CUSTOMER 1
> The Leaf's the best music bar in this city, hands down.

> CUSTOMER 2
> Better than Preservation Hall?

> CUSTOMER 1
> Yeah, see, Preservation Hall's more of a venue. It closes early. The Leaf's open late. Most of those jazz musicians play at the Leaf, anyway.

> CUSTOMER 2
> Okay . . . Every time my wife and I visit, we stay close to the Quarter. It's easy!

> CUSTOMER 1
> (smiles)
> The Big Easy . . .

They toast and share a connection.

> CUSTOMER 2
> I'll check it out one day for sure.

Ramen finishes rinsing a pint glass.

> RAMEN
> *(to Dave)*

You still want the woman in red's phone number?

Dave lowers the book and looks at him.

> DAVE

I certainly do, sir. My libido is killing me today.

> RAMEN

T-M-I.

Dave turns around and continues reading.

Ramen gooses him.

> DAVE

Don't touch me!

Ramen laughs.

> RAMEN

Don't touch you?

> DAVE

You don't want to see me angry, Noodle!

> RAMEN

Love you!

> DAVE
> *(disarmed)*

You gonna give me the number?

Ramen takes the napkin out of his wallet.

Dave yanks it from him.

> RAMEN

Hey, easy tiger!

Dave uses it to mark his page in the book.

When are you gonna call her?

> DAVE

Tonight, after work.

> RAMEN

At midnight?

> DAVE

You'd be surprised . . . Now, do you mind? I'm only reading the greatest American novel ever written––

> RAMEN

Grapes of Wrath is better.

> DAVE
> *(scoffs)*

I got your grapes. How did it go with Jill on Friday night?

> RAMEN

She's great!

> DAVE
> *(a beat)*

Oh, I see . . . That's why you're giving me this phone number. Are you in love?

> RAMEN

C'mon.

DAVE
Wasn't your last girlfriend back in high
school or something? A cheerleader, right?

RAMEN
Ancient history.

DAVE
Whatever happened with that?

RAMEN
I don't know. She wanted me to keep going
with football. She and my dad really saw eye
to eye on that point. I got tired of it, I guess.

*Jill enters the bar. She's taken a real interest in Ramen, and it shows.
She's dressed to impress.*

She takes a seat at the bar.

Hi Jill!

JILL
What's up, Ray! How's the book Dave?

DAVE
Better than The Grapes of Wrath.

He gives Ramen a look.

Jill--best American novel--go!

JILL
Count of Monte Cristo?

DAVE
Wrong. That's a French novel.

RAMEN
--So what, good choice!
(aside; to Jill)
Moby-Dick was published in England first.

Dave overhears.

DAVE
No, it wasn't!
(mutters)
Whatever.

He continues reading.

RAMEN
(to Jill)
Have you read Monte Cristo in French?

JILL'S VOICE
(thinking)
Do the first couple chapters count?

JILL
Sure have.

RAMEN'S VOICE
(thinking)
Where has this woman been all my life?

RAMEN
Can I get you a drink?

JILL
Beer. I just left my late class--Medieval French History.

RAMEN
Ugh! Beer choice?

JILL

Grolsch?

He looks in the cooler.

RAMEN

Let's see . . . We have Grolsch.

He pulls out a Kronenbourg 1664 lager.

Sure you wouldn't rather a 1664, Frenchy?

JILL

I kinda prefer Dutch beers to French––Can
we go have dinner tonight?

RAMEN
(shyly)
I'm stuck here until midnight.

JILL

C'mon, you guys are so dead.

RAMEN
(to Dave)
Does . . . Dave think it's okay?

Ramen and Jill look over at Dave with sad puppy eyes.

DAVE
(lowers the book; shrugs)
Go ahead. I don't think anything special
is happening tonight. I can always call for
backup.

RAMEN
(triumphantly)
Yes! You're the man!

He climbs OVER the bar, disrupting the customers, and takes Jill by the hand.

They bolt to the front door.

> DAVE
> Don't climb over the bar . . .

But they're gone.

Dave checks on the same two customers still at the bar.

> You guys doing alright over here?

> CUSTOMER 1
> Oh, yeah, man! Wish that hot little number hadn't left.

> CUSTOMER 2
> *(nods in agreement)*
> I'll have another.

> CUSTOMER 1
> Same here . . . Hey, Dave, what's the best music bar in the city?

> DAVE
> House of Blues––

> CUSTOMER 1
> No way man––terrible view!

> DAVE
> Yeah, don't stand upstairs if it's sold out . . .

JACQUES enters the Shipwreck, and they all notice him walk up to the bar.

INSERT – WATCH

Dave checks the time, 6:48pm.

> DAVE
>
> Jacques! What's up, man? You close a little early?

> JACQUES
>
> No, I have to get back. I thought Ramen was working tonight.

> DAVE
>
> He just left with the new girl. They went to eat dinner somewhere.

> JACQUES
> *(smiles)*
>
> Good for him.

Jacques hands Dave a small, white ENVELOPE.

> Would you pass this along to him, David?

Dave turns it over.

He notices a red WAX STAMP of the Voodoo VEVE SYMBOL of a HEART PIERCED BY A DAGGER.

> DAVE
> *(to Jacques)*
>
> Of course, what is it?

> JACQUES
>
> It's an invitation to a voodoo ritual. Would you like to come, as well?

DAVE

I'm okay. Happy Ray talked to you though.
He's been having some weird dreams.

JACQUES

I hope we can help him find the answers he
seeks.

DAVE

Same, man . . . Well hey, I'll be here until
midnight if you care for a drink later. I'll get
this over to him.

JACQUES

Thanks.

INT. ITALIAN RESTAURANT – NIGHT

CLINK! They raise their glasses of RED WINE.

*Ramen and Jill are seated at a table inside a quaint Italian spot in the
French Quarter.*

RAMEN

For rescuing me from the Shipwreck!

JILL

Aye, matey!

They drink.

JUDAS sits alone, dining in a nearby booth but goes unseen by Ray.

A male WAITER approaches the table.

WAITER

Have we decided on entrees, y'all?

                    JILL
        Um, yes. The manicotti with Cajun shrimp
        sounds exquisite!

                    WAITER
                  (writing)
        One . . . manicotti.

Ramen's cell phone BUZZES in his pocket, and he checks it.

INSERT – PHONE SCREEN

A beat when he sees a text from Dave.

                  (to Ramen; casually)
        And for you, sir . . .

INSERT – PHOTO MESSAGE

We see a cell phone PHOTO of the envelope with the heart stamp. The MESSAGE: "Looks like you got invited to a voodoo ritual."

INSERT – TEXT REPLY

Ramen texts back: "Leave it by the register."

                    RAMEN
        --Yes, sorry! One sausage and pepperoni
        pizza, kind sir.

Jill smiles.

                    WAITER
        Okay, thanks!

The waiter takes their MENUS and heads off.

                    RAMEN
        You caught me off guard tonight.

JILL
(sinisterly; joking)
My plan is working.

RAMEN
(smiles)
How were you able to get away from studying?

JILL
Well Ramen, I do study French, and I'm basically fluent so––

RAMEN
(nods in agreement)
So, French is your passion huh?

JILL
You could say that again!

RAMEN
How did you know?

JILL
It's been that way since I was a kid. I had a French tutor, starting at age eight. I think it was the society thing to do at the time . . . Anyway, I got to visit Paris on a school trip in junior high, and I fell in love with it!

RAMEN
I see. Why not go study there?

JILL
'Cause I'm an American. Maybe eventually–– there's always grad school. How about you? Is writing something you're passionate about?

RAMEN

I've wanted to be a writer for a long time, so
... yeah.

JILL

Why?

RAMEN

My parents used to fight a lot. And I felt like
I had a lot to say but couldn't. It was like I
found this magical way to express myself.

JILL

Writing is definitely therapeutic. I wrote in a
diary during tougher times, growing up.

RAMEN

Diary's a lost art.

JILL

A diary's one thing though. A career in sto-
rytelling is another ... You don't think you're
holding onto something, do you?

RAMEN

Straight shooter, huh?

Jill raises her glass in agreement.

Maybe I was holding on at first. But then it
kept evolving. People started to tell me I was
good at it. I listened, that's all.

JILL

You might be special ...

RAMEN
(*smirks*)
As in "rides the short bus?"

JILL
(laughing)
No, stupid! As in being an artist.
(sighs)
Can we talk about New Orleans, Mr. Artist?

RAMEN
Ray. Or I'm afraid my head will explode.

JILL
Okay, Ray. I love how this city never sleeps!

RAMEN
I thought that was New York.

JILL
No--some bars are open late in New York City, like 4am, but you can't actually sit on a barstool and watch the sunrise anywhere.

RAMEN
I still don't know how people do that . . . But, they do. My cousin Mackie works the early shift--

JILL
At The Shipwreck?

RAMEN
Yeah.

JILL
Nepotism?

RAMEN
Networking. He doesn't own the bar! And what makes you think I didn't get him the job?

       JILL

Did you?

      RAMEN

No.

       JILL
      (smirks)
I'm messing with you, kinda . . .

      RAMEN

Anyway . . . He says a handful of people are usually still there from the night before when he goes in.

       JILL

God . . . Loaded, I bet!

      RAMEN

Interview with a vampire.

They laugh.

       JILL

Do you go out?

      RAMEN

Sometimes. It's fun working in the Quarter. When I'm there I feel like I'm out, you know. Customers like to buy me a shot and tell me their stories.

       JILL
      (shrugs)
Yeah, but work is still work. What do you do for fun?

RAMEN

I watch a ton of movies. Read. I love music, watching the Saints--You?

JILL

At risk of sounding cliche for a woman, cooking--French cuisine.

RAMEN

The best.

JILL

The fucking best! I also like traveling. I went to Japan like a year ago with my parents-- probably why I think your name is funny-- and it is . . . I also enjoy sports and music. Did you play sports growing up?

RAMEN

Oh, yeah. I was pretty good at football. I played offense. In fact, my dad disowned me after I turned down a football scholarship.

JILL

Oh, God. That's terrible!

RAMEN

What part?

JILL

That your dad doesn't accept you.

RAMEN

He's like super-alpha macho. He coached me when I was growing up. In a way, it's some of the best times and some of the worst. I hated how he took it so seriously . . . He wanted to be a football player more than I ever did.

JILL

Can I tell you something?

RAMEN

Of course!

JILL

You're not like a typical football player.

RAMEN

I'm not a football player at all.

JILL

Right. But I mean you look athletic, although there's something else going on. You seem——smart.

RAMEN

I studied.

ANOTHER TOAST

JILL

To studying.

RAMEN

Cheers!

JILL

If it's any consolation, it sounds like me and my mom. She had a freaking building named after her for being a great surgeon. Yet, here I am, in New Orleans.

RAMEN

——Being your own person, despite the odds.

JILL
(smiles)
Do you ever try to call your dad?

RAMEN
I'll call him one day when I have something to rub in his goddam face. Next subject, please.

JILL
Okay–– Did you write anything over the weekend?

RAMEN
I started a new screenplay actually. I wrote most of the weekend. I think you inspired me.

A beat as we see Judas walking past their table, and Ray catches a glimpse of his face before he exits the restaurant.

JILL
Tell me more!

RAMEN
(startled)
. . . Well, it's supposed to be for my writing capstone. That's all I have left for my English degree.

JILL
Mon Dieu! Lucky guy! I have almost two years left!

RAMEN
(shrugs)
I struggle with this class, though. It makes me worry.

JILL

How?

RAMEN

Maybe it's my teacher. Everything's money money money!
(sips)
Whatever, I'm gonna show him, too.

JILL

So much to prove--

RAMEN

Yep. When I finish the new script, I'm going to sell it.

JILL

That's the spirit!

RAMEN
(smirks)
To be honest, it might never happen.

JILL

Why?

RAMEN

It feels like there's too much luck involved.

JILL
(a beat)
Good thing you're lucky . . .

RAMEN

Can we get drunk tonight and forget about the future?

JILL

As you wish--You ever seen The Princess
Bride?

RAMEN
(excitedly)
I love The Princess Bride! Like when he's
tumbling down the hill and screaming, "As
Youuuu Wiiishh!"

They laugh.

JILL

--So funny!

The waiter arrives with their entrees.

Ramen raises a glass of wine to his MOUTH for a sip.

JUMP CUT TO:

INT. JILL'S BEDROOM – NIGHT

*A murky green ABSINTHE glass is lowered from Ramen's MOUTH,
after a sip.*

*They sit on a RUG in front of her BED while "Midnight in a Perfect
World" by DJ Shadow plays on the radio.*

*The two face each other with a box of SUGAR CUBES, a PITCHER
of water, a BOTTLE of LUCID absinthe, and two GLASSES poured
between them.*

*The layout of her apartment is similar to Ramen's: minimal, but it has
a warmer touch in decor.*

INSERT – POSTER

She has a framed classic 1939 movie POSTER of The Hunchback of

Notre Dame.

INSERT – PHOTO
With her PARENTS in front of a JAPANESE TEMPLE on a DESK.

> RAMEN
> This is so thoughtful! You shouldn't have.

> JILL
> *(shrugs)*
> Occupational development.

> RAMEN
> Oh, bartending research? Don't mind if I do.

He sips.

> Tastes like licorice.
> *(chuckles)*
> Am I the only person who likes licorice?

> JILL
> Not anymore!

They laugh, firing on all cylinders.

> Know any classic toasts?

Ray thinks, then raises his glass:

> RAMEN
> May you be in heaven a half hour before the
> devil knows you're dead.

> JILL
> Nice! How about this? To the green fairy,
> and her notorious past!

TOAST – ABSINTHE

Clink!

Ramen puts his glass down. He pulls a JOINT from his shirt pocket.

> RAMEN
> Speaking of a notorious past, how dumb is marijuana law!

> JILL
> Is that weed?

> RAMEN
> Want to get stoned?

> JILL
> (sighs)
> Sure. But full disclosure: it usually makes me hungry and sleepy.

> RAMEN
> As long as it doesn't make you go crazy . . .

He lights the joint, and they pass it back and forth during the following conversation:

> JILL
> Tell me more about your movie.

> RAMEN
> Do you remember I told you that I had a voodoo dream the other night?

Jill nods.

> It was really dark. It had this gigantic guy.
> He was wearing an alligator mask.

       JILL
      (exhales)

A monster . . .

      RAMEN

Oh, it gets worse. He's dragging this dead high school football player through the woods.

       JILL

Total horror––

      RAMEN

Then he puts the body on an altar––like a voodoo altar or something. He drinks the guy's blood and eats him!

After a moment, Jill laughs.

       JILL

And now you're writing a horror movie based on a nightmare?

      RAMEN

Yes.

       JILL
      (a beat)
Jesus! Are you the football player?

Ramen inhales the joint and blows out smoke.

      RAMEN

What?

       JILL

Well, yeah I mean . . . maybe this sacrifice is

you for writing a movie or something?

He passes it to Jill, and he scoots over to lean against the foot of her bed.

RAMEN
––I hadn't thought of that.

JILL
Yeah, think about it. Are you sacrificing anything?

RAMEN
Time.

JILL
Yeah ... Time is all we've got.

She laughs. The pot is kicking in.

RAMEN
It's funny, but you're kind of blowing my
mind right now!

JILL
I'm stoned, Ray. I don't know what I'm
talking about ...

RAMEN
No, I think you're really insightful, actually.
Remember that skinny guy that came to the
bar on Friday?

JILL
Yeah, how could I forget!

RAMEN
Right. He's totally nice––

JILL
(*an epiphany*)
Oh, you were telling him about the dream! That makes sense. I was thinking, "What the hell are they talking about?"

Ramen laughs.

RAMEN
That guy invited me to a voodoo ritual. He said it could help me figure out my dreams.

JILL
Whoa! That sounds like The Twilight Zone. Are you going to a voodoo ritual?

RAMEN
(*pauses*)
I don't know. Dave sent me a text. I got my invite tonight. I kinda need help sorting things out . . .

Jill nods.

To be honest I've been feeling a little hopeless.

JILL
Why?

RAMEN
Because . . . I'm failing my class. I'm either going to graduate or not. And then what? It's starting to feel like I'm on a treadmill, and my dream of becoming a screenwriter is getting further away each day . . . Until this weekend, writing was starting to feel like a

distant fantasy.

                    JILL
                  (smiles)
If you're a writer, then it's what you're meant
to do in my opinion. It's your dream, Ray.
School can only prepare you so much. At
some point you gotta make the jump.

                    RAMEN
I know. But it's not like every writer makes it.

                    JILL
You gotta go for it, and you can't lose hope
. . . What the hell are we without dreams,
anyway?

*He leans over to kiss her. She meets him halfway for a PASSIONATE
KISS.*

*She scoots next to him against the foot of the bed and rests her head
on his shoulder.*

                  (sighs)
I want you to sleep over.

                    RAMEN
                  (faces her)
Okay.

                    JILL
                  (faces him)
But, I'm gonna ask for a rain check because I
have French Lit early in the morning.

                RAMEN'S VOICE
                  (thinking)
I didn't see that coming.

> RAMEN
> *(frowns)*

A rain check?

> JILL

Don't look sad. It's our first date!

> RAMEN

I'm not sad.

> JILL

Good! We could go for coffee tomorrow after my class if you want?

> RAMEN
> *(smiles)*

I like coffee.

INT. RAMEN'S BEDROOM – NIGHT

Ramen has returned home and lies in bed, alone.

> RAMEN
> *(sighs)*
> Jill Lafon. What a babe!

His EYES remain open for another moment before he falls asleep.

EXT. RURAL SUBDIVISION – NIGHT (A DREAM)

JUDAS drives the ANTIQUE TRUCK up a thin highway, miles away from the city of New Orleans. Again, "Heebie Jeebies," by Louis Armstrong plays on the radio.

He passes by the front gate of a MANSION on acres of land. The gate bears the family name: BROWNSTONE.

INT. ANTIQUE TRUCK – NIGHT

The ALLIGATOR MASK and the GLOWING BOX are next to Judas

on the passenger seat.

He veers off of the highway and parks the TRUCK in a discrete area behind an abandoned TRAILER HOME.

EXT. ABANDONED TRAILER HOME – NIGHT

A beat as the alligator BOOT steps out of the truck.

The MANSION sits in the distance on the adjacent property. Judas deftly hops a FENCE and walks toward it.

INT. MANSION KITCHEN – NIGHT

Judas uses a dagger to open the BACKDOOR.

HIS POV

Through the mask as he STEALTHILY closes the backdoor. It appears to be a KITCHEN. He looks from side to side. It's dark inside, and quiet … Except for a WHITE CAT that meows and runs off.

INT. MANSION FOYER – NIGHT

He quietly enters the dark, vacant foyer and ascends a winding STAIRCASE.

INT. MANSION HALLWAY – NIGHT

Upstairs, the monster reaches an open bedroom door. The lights are out, and someone is heard SNORING.

He pauses in the doorway for a moment before continuing further down the hall.

He reaches another door at the end of the hall that is CLOSED.

INT. SHEILA'S BEDROOM – NIGHT

Sheila lies fast asleep on top of the covers, hugging a pillow, wearing a T-SHIRT and panties.

She left a CD playing "Fade Into You" by Mazzy Star, softly.

In her spacious, TIDY bedroom, she has an '06 GRADUATION CAP on her DRESSER and PHOTOGRAPHS on her walls—of the CHEERLEADING TEAM, a SENIOR PORTRAIT, and a PROM DANCE PHOTO with Randall that is labeled "Sheila and Randy Forever."

The monster opens her bedroom door. It squeaks a little. He pauses in the DOORWAY, the light behind him making one hell of a SILHOUETTE.

HIS POV

As he approaches the sleeping beauty. He puts his hand on her. She AWAKENS for a MOMENT and GASPS, but before she can scream, he covers her mouth with a CHLOROFORM RAG, and she's back asleep.

EXT. TRAILWAY – NIGHT

TEARS run from Sheila's eyes. Her mouth is tied with a HANDKERCHIEF. Judas holds her tightly over his shoulder and walks down the trail. She's upside down, helpless, and terrified.

She is SHACKLED with IRONS at her hands and feet, and she's BLEEDING where they are digging into her skin.

She tries to speak but can only manage muffled CRIES.

She pounds on his back with clad hands . . . Nothing.

He turns his head and looks at her. She releases a muffled shriek.

He laughs.

JUDAS
(severely)

Don't struggle so hard.

SHEILA
(muffled)
What-ith-thith! What-ith-thith!

JUDAS
All of your ambitions will cease very soon.

SHEILA
(sobbing)
Thto-o-o-o-p. Ple-e-e-ase!

He continues steadily down the dark trail.

EXT. WORSHIP SITE – NIGHT

They reach the clearing, and the voodoo box begins glowing red on the altar.

CANDLES on the altar IGNITE automatically.

When he drops her on the altar, she hits her head and is stunned.

He sets down the glowing box on the ground next to the altar.

SUDDENLY Sheila comes to her senses. She hits him with clasped hands hard enough to knock off the alligator mask, revealing his face.

Her eyes grow wide. Does she recognize him?

SHEILA
(muffled)
Father? Judath?

He places the alligator mask back on his head.

(crying)
Nooo-o-o-o-o!

Angrily, he LOCKS her wrists to the altar above her head.

He fastens her ankles to the altar so her legs are spread apart.

JUDAS
You choose to suffer.

HIS POV

As he wipes a tear from her eye, and she winces.

He squeezes her mouth, causing her to dry heave.

He unsheathes the DAGGER.

Candlelight and the red glow of the box grows brighter.

She looks desperately toward the sky.

SHEILA'S VOICE
HELP ME!!

Her plea reaches the TREETOPS, then the COSMOS, and the dream ends.

INT./EXT. RAMEN'S BEDROOM – DAY

Down from the COSMOS, to the apartment ROOFTOP to RAMEN asleep in bed, the plea for help is heard, and Ramen's EYES pop open.

He takes a DEEP BREATH.

INSERT – DATE
Tuesday, April 17, 2007

He stands up and stretches, shirtless, wearing boxer shorts.

He notices leaves and muddy footprints on the floor, leading to the other side of the bed.

And he finally notices a blond woman in her birthday suit lying asleep under the covers.

He squints. Was she there all night?

He clears his throat.

The woman turns over looking somewhat haggard and dirty, but still a beauty. It's Sheila.

RAMEN
(agitatedly)

Hi! Um . . . Who are you? And what are you
doing in my bed?

She awakens softly to see Ray standing there. She's no longer shack-led, but her WRISTS and ANKLES eerily show scrapes and bruises.

She sits up, pulling the sheet over her bust.

SHEILA
(yawning)

What are you so wound up about?

RAMEN

What? What do you mean? Who are you?

SHEILA

I'm Sheila Brownstone. I'm from your
dream, Ray. I called for you. You brought me
here last night.

RAMEN
(loudly)

That doesn't make any sense! What are you

talking about?

                    SHEILA
You don't need to yell!

She notices her dirty arms and bruises.

Oh, God, I need a bath. I'm a total mess . . .

She stands up while pulling the sheet over her body. Ramen doesn't know whether to scream or fall in love.

                    (pointing)
Is that the bathroom?

He nods.

She walks OFF-SCREEN to the bathroom, and he hears her running a BATH.

Then, a KNOCK on the front door.

                    RAMEN
                    (startled)
Who is it?

                    JILL (O.S.)
Hey it's Jill! Good, you're awake!

                    RAMEN
                    (to himself)
Oh, no!
                    (to Jill)
Hey, I'm a little busy now. Can you come back later?

INTERCUT

With Jill outside at the front door:

JILL

Okaay--

(pauses)

What are you doing? I thought you wanted
to get coffee.

RAMEN

I do . . . I just . . . I'm writing.

JILL

Were you writing all night?

RAMEN'S VOICE
(thinking)
God, why won't she go away?

RAMEN

Yep, I'm right in the middle of it.

JILL

That's intense, Ray!

RAMEN

Sure is!

JILL

I got out of class a little early, and I wanted
to see you--

He opens the front door and stands in the doorway.

RAMEN

Hi.

JILL

Hey, hot stuff!

RAMEN

Look, I would love to have coffee with you, like so much, but it's just not a good time right now.

JILL
(smiles)
Aw, Ray, you need a break . . . I'm a little hungover, too. Last night was fun.

RAMEN
(sighs)
I really liked last night.

He hears WATER SPLASHING and looks nervously at the bathroom door.

SHEILA (O.S.)
I feel better already! Thanks, Ray!

RAMEN
(to Jill; nervously)
Can I meet you a little later?

JILL
Are you really in the middle of it?

RAMEN
Yes! I just . . . I have to get it all down before it leaves my head, forever.

JILL
(pouty)
So I can't come in?

RAMEN
Jill—

                    (pauses)
Look, somewhere between last night and
this morning I entered The Twilight Zone.

She laughs.

                     JILL
You're so cute. What are you talking about?

She sniffs him and winces.

Take a quick shower. I'll wait.

                    RAMEN
No! I mean, okay . . . Come on in!

Jill enters the apartment for the first time, and it's a mess: clothes, dirty dishes, full ashtrays.

He dashes for the bathroom and slams the door.

                 RAMEN (O.S.)
Sorry about the mess!

She notices that his LAPTOP is closed on his desk.

                 JILL'S VOICE
                    (thinking)
That's weird.

                 RAMEN (O.S.)
I'll be right out!

                     JILL
Didn't you say you were writing––

RAMEN'S BATHROOM

He sees Sheila leaning back in the tub. Her head rests above thick BUBBLES.

SHEILA
You have a visitor?

RAMEN
(whispers)
Yeah, time like this!

RAMEN'S BEDROOM
Jill walks to the bathroom door and leans her ear against it.

RAMEN (O.S.)
(whispers)
You need to go away!

Jill knocks.

JILL
Ramen, are you talking to someone?

RAMEN (O.S.)
(pauses)
Why would I––no!

JILL'S VOICE
(thinking)
Just talking to yourself, no big deal . . .

JILL
Are you sure? Sounded like you were talking
to someone.

She barges in.

RAMEN'S BATHROOM

JILL'S POV

As Ramen shrieks, quickly steps into the bathtub, and drags the curtain across. She walks over and peeks behind the curtain: She cannot see Sheila—only Ramen, standing in his boxer shorts in the corner, covering his face in a cringe.

RAMEN'S POV

As he slowly turns, peeking through his fingers at Jill. He looks down at Sheila sitting in the bath below and back up at Jill.

                    RAMEN
          I can explain.

                    JILL
          Explain why you're looking like I'm about to
          murder you?

Lips tightened, he points down at the tub.

JILL'S POV

Dry, empty tub.

                    (a beat)
          Oh, I get it . . . It's actually cleaner than mine,
          Ray! Propre, en Français.

                    RAMEN
                    (delicately)
          Huh?

                    JILL
          . . . Are we on the same page today?

He shrugs.

Ray, it sounded like you were talking to someone, so I came in. I'm very sorry. I'm gonna go sit on your bed while you finish up.

Shocked, he nods.

Jill exits the bathroom.

He hops out of the tub and shuts the door behind her.

He turns to see Sheila scrubbing a bruised and cut ANKLE above the bubbles.

She smiles at him.

SHEILA

That was close, huh?

RAMEN'S BEDROOM

Ramen comes out of the bathroom hot.

Jill stands looking at his writing awards on the wall.

JILL
(*frankly*)

You didn't shower.

RAMEN

I can't make it to coffee this morning. I really need you to go.

He walks to the front door and opens it.

JILL

. . . Something's up. You said you were writing, but your computer's not even on.

RAMEN

Look, no offense, but what do you know about writing?

JILL
(swallows)
Nothing, I guess. Is everything okay?

RAMEN

It's fine.

JILL'S VOICE
(thinking)
Everything is so not fine.

He motions for her to leave.

JILL
(upset)

I'm leaving!

She walks out.

INT./EXT. RAMEN'S APARTMENT – CONTINUOUS

Jill turns around on the DOORSTEP to face him.

Ramen stands in the doorway.

RAMEN
(sighs)
I'm sorry. I'll call you later. It's just, The Fucking Twilight Zone right now.

JILL
Do whatever you want.

He shuts the door on her.

                      (loudly)
    Bye Ramen!
                      (to herself)
    Seriously?

She walks away unhappily.

RAMEN'S BATHROOM

Sheila stands in front of the mirror, wrapped underneath her arms in a WHITE bath towel, another towel wrapped around her head, brushing her teeth.

She turns and looks at Ramen, who's standing in the doorway.

                  SHEILA
           (muffled by toothbrush)
    What's wrong?

He takes a deep breath.

                  RAMEN
    What's wrong? Oh, my God!
              (claps)
    I need answers. Please!

She spits in the sink and puts down the toothbrush.

                  SHEILA
    You have the answers.

He shows distress, almost a sob.

                  RAMEN
    No--I--don't.

                  SHEILA
    Try, Ray.

He settles down some.

> RAMEN
>
> Okay. Your name is Sheila, right? Sheila Brownstone?

> SHEILA
>
> Yes.

> RAMEN
>
> And you're from my dream?

> SHEILA
> *(nodding)*
>
> Yes.

> RAMEN
>
> How is that possible if I'm awake? I'm awake, aren't I?

She pinches his arm.

> Ouch!

> SHEILA
>
> You're awake.

> RAMEN
>
> Do that again.

A MIRROR

We only see Ray, pinching himself.

> Am I crazy?

> SHEILA
>
> I'm just here to help you move the plot along

in your monster movie.

RAMEN'S VOICE
(thinking)
I'm talking to a character from my script.

SHEILA
You're probably not the first.

RAMEN
You can hear my thoughts?

SHEILA
I am your thoughts.

RAMEN'S VOICE
(thinking)
I don't have any white bath towels, do I?

She leans in closely.

SHEILA
(softly)
That doesn't matter, Ramen. I only live in your imagination.

He covers his mouth in disbelief and exits the bathroom.

She turns around and re-fastens her towel.

RAMEN'S BEDROOM

Ramen dresses hastily in shorts and a V-neck. He picks up some tennis shoes.

SHEILA (O.S.)
What are you doing?

He sits on the edge of the bed to put them on and tie them.

RAMEN
I have to go to the bar to pick up an envelope
. . . I don't know, are you coming?

Sheila enters the room.

SHEILA
Sure, how's this?

He looks up from his shoes.

She stands in front of him, wearing a crop top T-shirt, cutoff shorts, and tennis shoes.

RAMEN
You look like an actress in a horror movie.

INT. THE SHIPWRECK BAR, FRENCH QUARTER – DAY

Ramen and Sheila enter the Shipwreck together.

Ramen's cousin MACKIE works during the day: cool and tan like a surfer. He's stocky with long brown hair and a goatee.

Sheila plays "Mr. Brownstone" by Guns N' Roses on the jukebox, but Mackie only sees Ray standing there.

The bar is empty except for a middle-aged LOCAL DRUNK man paying his tab.

MACKIE
(to local drunk)
Be careful in those mean streets, Jack!

The drunk heads away from the bar, wobbly.

LOCAL DRUNK
(raspy)
Thanks, Mackie!

The man exits.

Mackie's really happy to see Ramen. It's been ages.

MACKIE
Staaaabaaaaaaah! What's up my brother!

Ramen gives Mackie a big hug across the bar.

Sheila takes a seat on a barstool next to Ramen.

RAMEN
Living the dream. What's up Stab-ah? You good?

MACKIE
Can't complain. Miss you! Heard you have a new girlfriend.

RAMEN
Damn, word travels.

MACKIE
Small town.
(pauses)
Maybe a little early for G'N'R, Ray.

RAMEN
. . . I didn't play this.

MACKIE
(confused)
You weren't just standing at the jukebox?

Ray looks at Sheila.

She shrugs.

> RAMEN
> *(to Mackie)*
> Oh––yeah . . . Figured you needed a little early jolt!

> MACKIE
> It's all good. I think you might have scared old Jack . . . Oh, well! I think he's been here for like eight hours!

> RAMEN
> I'm glad I got here before he sucked all your blood.

> MACKIE
> *(smirks)*
> Poor dude's lonely. Tips well.

> RAMEN
> Just hope he doesn't drive . . .

> MACKIE
> Nah––super-local.

> RAMEN
> . . . I think there's an envelope here for me.

> MACKIE
> An envelope?

> RAMEN
> Yeah, Dave said it would be here. It should have a little heart symbol on it.

Mackie checks near the REGISTER.

                         MACKIE
                         (looking)
          Heart symbol . . . A love letter?

                         RAMEN
          No. It's from Jacques. It's an invite to a voo-
          doo ritual.

                         MACKIE
          Voodoo? No shit.

He finds the envelope, hands it to Ray.

          This prolly it right here.

                         RAMEN
          That's it.

Ramen opens the envelope and pulls out the INVITATION.

INSERT – INVITATION

"Ancestor's of Marie Laveau Ritual Invite: Friday, 9pm." In handwrit-
ten script beneath, "The spirits have the answers you seek, Ramen.
Meet me at the shop around closing time, if you're still interested. —
Jacques Gautreaux"

                         MACKIE
          . . . You ought to come see me more, lil cous-
          in. You've been writing, I hope?

                         RAMEN
          Yeah, man. Trying to write a new mov-
          ie––something about voodoo. Mom knows
          someone. I may have a shot.

MACKIE

Killer! Marie Laveau biopic?

RAMEN

No . . . Alligator Man.

Sheila rolls her eyes.

MACKIE

Gator-man!
(a beat)
Don't kill yourself, stab-ah. You hear? Take care of things. Do what's in front of you.

RAMEN

Thanks Mackie . . . miss you.

MACKIE

Miss you too! Don't be a stranger––I gotta meet this new girl!

RAMEN

You bet.

Mackie gives Ramen another big hug.

Love you, man.

MACKIE

Love you too, my brother!

EXT. THE SHIPWRECK BAR, FRENCH QUARTER – DAY

Sheila follows Ramen across the street toward Jacques' voodoo shop.

SHEILA

He's really sweet.

RAMEN
The best.

SUDDENLY a DUMP TRUCK comes flying past Ray. Sheila doesn't get out the way in time . . .

Sheila!

The truck passes, and she's gone.

She reappears behind him, unharmed, and startles him.

SHEILA
That guy's gonna kill somebody!

Ramen jumps.

RAMEN
Don't do that! . . . You know? You still seem real or something.

A female PASSERBY stops to look at Ramen, who's talking and gesturing to thin air.

(to Sheila)
I'm not used to this, OKAY?

He notices the passerby staring at him.

(to passerby)
I'm not crazy!
PASSERBY
Sure.

She keeps walking.

EXT. VOODOO GIFT SHOP – CONTINUOUS

Ray and Sheila reach the familiar display window of the voodoo shop, and he peers inside.

Jacques is behind the counter.

>   SHEILA
>   Can I say one thing?

>   RAMEN
>   Yeah, go ahead.

>   SHEILA
>   Your movie sucks.

He faces her.

>   RAMEN
>   (scoffs)
>   What? I'm working my butt off! You're just a
>   voice in my head. Now quiet!

Ramen knocks on the window and gets Jacques' attention.

He holds up the invitation and gives Jacques a THUMBS UP.

Jacques smiles and returns the gesture.

>   SHEILA
>   I mean . . . How would you like it if you were
>   about to be sacrificed on an altar?

Ray looks at her.

>   RAMEN
>   Go away.

                    SHEILA
You think you'll get rich and famous if you
write a movie?

                    RAMEN
Hope so! And while I'm at it, show my dad,
my teachers, and anyone else how a small-
time kid from New Orleans made it big.

                    SHEILA
                 (a beat)
The only way to make it happen is to finish
your screenplay.

Ray laughs.

What? I'm right! What's so funny?

                    RAMEN
Nothing, it's just--my professor. He said I
lack imagination ...
                 (laughs)
And now my imagination is talking to me in
the middle of the Quarter--What time is it?

                    SHEILA
Noon.

                    RAMEN
C'mon. I owe Green a visit.

Another DUMP TRUCK passes by loudly and distracts Ray.

He looks again, and Sheila is no longer there.

Sheila?

                    (to himself)
Shit.

INT. UNIVERSITY FACULTY HALLWAY – DAY

Ramen approaches Professor Green's OFFICE DOOR.

He hears Sara Bishop's voice on the other side.

                    SARA BISHOP (O.S.)
So you really think I have what it takes, huh?

                    PROFESSOR GREEN (O.S.)
Absolutely! I think you might be the brightest student I've taught in years. And I will recommend you for film school.

Ramen knocks.

Who is it?

                    RAMEN
Ray Noodle, sir.

                    PROFESSOR GREEN (O.S.)
We're almost finished!

Another moment and the DOOR OPENS. Sara Bishop heads out.

She and Ray exchange cold GLANCES.

She looks back at Professor Green sitting behind his DESK and smiles.

Have a great day, Sara! Talk to you soon.

                    SARA BISHOP
Thanks Eddie! Bye!

PROFESSOR GREEN

Come on in, Ramen.

PROFESSOR GREEN'S OFFICE

Ramen enters the cozy faculty office, and soft, classical piano by Frédéric Chopin plays on a CD.

Professor Green stands to greet him from behind a desk with a firm HANDSHAKE.

They both take a seat.

PROFESSOR GREEN

What can I do for you?

RAMEN

I came to say that I'm working on a new screenplay, sir.

PROFESSOR GREEN

Hope it's not another romance! It's not your strong suit.

RAMEN

No, sir. This is a horror.

PROFESSOR GREEN

"Oh, the horror."
(smirks)
I mean, horror movies get made all the time. They don't even have to be good!

RAMEN'S VOICE
(thinking)

Did he just––

PROFESSOR GREEN

So, you've started a new script, hopefully?

RAMEN

I have.

PROFESSOR GREEN

Good. How can I help?

RAMEN
(struggles)

W-well, I'm experiencing s-something new, um, as of late, um––Where do ideas come from?

PROFESSOR GREEN

The Muses, to the Ancient Greeks. Jung called it the daemon, our individual driving force, always whispering inspiration. To guys like us . . . I don't know, probably somewhere in the middle of our brains. From all sorts of places, I guess. What's that word?

He snaps his finger.

Imagination.

He smiles.

I hope this new script has some better ideas going on than "Heat Index," son . . . What, are you––lonely?

RAMEN
(defensively)

––I'm dating someone.

Green nods.

I wasn't though, before.

PROFESSOR GREEN

That explains things . . . It's just that after a
certain point, sex on film becomes boring.
Kubrick knew that. You'll notice it when we
watch A Clockwork Orange coming up in
class. Godard, a French director, once said
all you need to make a movie is a girl and a
gun. See, you have to balance out sex with
violence. Then, they're hooked.

RAMEN

I understand.

PROFESSOR GREEN

I know you do. It's that tiny, lizard part of our
brains, son . . . the part that won't let us look
away, even if we want to.

Professor Green checks his WATCH.

Anything else? How much do you have written for this new horror script?

RAMEN

Twenty pages?

PROFESSOR GREEN

Good!

RAMEN

Yeah, so basically, this alligator monster
wants to sacrifice this young couple to some
evil voodoo spirit––

Professor Green interrupts Ramen by standing up.

What are you doing?

PROFESSOR GREEN
Time's up. Get out there and make it happen!

RAMEN
Wait, I'm not finished! I haven't even told you about my dreams!

PROFESSOR GREEN
Dreams? I don't have time to talk about Freud with you right now . . . Look, I want you to succeed. You may not believe me, but I do . . . I want you to move on to bigger and better things after graduation. Perhaps more to the point, I don't want you taking my class again.

RAMEN
I don't want to retake the class.

PROFESSOR GREEN
Then level with me, here—I'm asking for a minimal effort from you to graduate. Then, you can resume your career as a bartender or whatever amazing life choices you make from there on out.

RAMEN
I need help. I'm confused . . . Do you not like me?

PROFESSOR GREEN
(sighs)
The truth? I might not like you . . . I'll tell you a secret: I don't like most of my students. You kinda fit into that category. Another kid with wide eyes and no clue how the world works.

                          RAMEN
            Are you kidding me?

The classical music TEMPO PICKS UP, the track changes to "Hungarian Dance No. 5" by Johannes Brahms.

                     PROFESSOR GREEN
            I'm not kidding, Ramen. Graduation is in
            one month. Go home and make your two lit-
            tle index fingers type something that makes
            enough sense for me to pass you ... capisce?

                          RAMEN
                        (deflated)
            Capisce.

Ramen stands.

Professor Green places a hand on his back and ushers him towards the door in haste:

                     PROFESSOR GREEN
            Alright, welp, have a good one!

He opens the door.

Ramen turns around in the middle of the doorway, just as the classical tune CRESCENDOS.

                          RAMEN
            Wait! My imagination is alive! It talks to me,
            and I don't know how to control it!

                     PROFESSOR GREEN
            Of course your imagination has come to life!
            You're in my class!

                    RAMEN
    I'm scared!

                PROFESSOR GREEN
                   (smirks)
    Then go see a priest! Office hours are over,
    Ramen. See you in class!

He shuts the door in Ray's face.

UNIVERSITY FACULTY HALLWAY – CONTINUOUS

Ray rests his head against Green's office door for a moment.

                    RAMEN
       Ugh.

*He walks away from the office down the hall. A SUDDEN BEAT as
Ray passes one faculty office door on the way out, and we see the alligator man's head in the window, watching him.*

INT. RAMEN'S BEDROOM – DAY

*Ramen sits at the desk in front of his computer, preparing a glass of
glowing ABSINTHE: glass, spoon, sugar cube . . .*

INSERT – DATE

Thursday, April 19, 2007

*. . . absinthe, water . . . He drinks. SHEILA lies on his bed, READING
A BOOK ABOUT VOODOO. "Don't Stop Believin'" plays, and Ramen
answers his cell phone.*

                    RAMEN
       Yo!

                  MOM'S VOICE
    Ramen?

INT. MOM'S HOUSE – DAY

Ramen's mom sits comfortably on her sofa, watching SOAP OPERAS on television.

She turns down the TV volume with a remote.

INTERCUT

With Ramen sitting at his desk.

> RAMEN
>
> Hey mom, what's up? I'm kinda busy, writing my screenplay.

> MOM
>
> That's why I'm calling. Listen, my friend I was telling you about in the movie industry is really interested in your screenplay. He works for Everest Films. Ever heard of them?

> RAMEN
>
> Everest Films? Duh, they're like top-three!

> MOM
>
> I figured you would know. He says they love all that voodoo stuff, and they're short for their Halloween lineup over the next year or two. And they're shooting movies in New Orleans next year. He says he can get your script in front of the right people.

> RAMEN
>
> Really?

> MOM
> (smiles)
>
> Really!

He jumps up. Sheila signals a ROCK AND ROLL hand salute.

RAMEN

Oh my God! That's great! I . . . still have work
to do. But, I mean, when does he need it by?

MOM

Is two weeks enough time? He said so and so
is coming in town for a meeting on May 3rd
and he'd like to have something for then.

He takes a sip of the cloudy absinthe . . .

INT. COLLEGE CLASSROOM – DAY (FLASHBACK)

Ramen recalls a key piece of a classroom lecture by Professor Green.

PROFESSOR GREEN
(to class)

Let me tell you the story of how I wrote the
best screenplay of my life in one weekend . . .

BACK TO:

RAMEN'S BEDROOM

Ramen checks the page count on his script. He's on page 50.

MOM'S VOICE

. . . Ray? You still there?

RAMEN

Yes! Two weeks is fine. I can do it.

INTERCUT – MOM'S HOUSE

Still lounging.

MOM

You sure? I mean you don't want to blow it.

> RAMEN

I'll do my best.

> MOM

That's all you can do. LEGO's, son! One piece at a time. Get to work!

> RAMEN

Okay, love you, mom!

> MOM

Love you, noodle-head. Good luck! Mom believes in you!

She puts the phone down, and then turns the TV volume back up with the remote.

INT. THE SHIPWRECK BAR – NIGHT

A handful of people are seated in booths, merrily drinking and talking while "Frontwards" by Pavement plays on the jukebox.

Ramen wipes the bar with a towel.

Dave leans against the back counter, reading Moby-Dick.

> RAMEN

You haven't finished that, yet?

> DAVE

I work Ramen. It's not always conducive to leisure.

Ramen pretends he's going to crack Dave with his towel.

Can't I read in peace?

Ramen cracks him.

Ouch! You'll pay for that! What are you so hyped about, anyway?

RAMEN
Apparently, I have a foot in the door with one the world's biggest movie companies.

DAVE
How's that?

RAMEN
Mom knows someone, and that someone knows a big someone.

DAVE
You gonna show them your romance script?

RAMEN
––Think voodoo.

DAVE
The Alligator Man, you finished it?

RAMEN
Not exactly, but it's coming along. I have two weeks.

DAVE
Two weeks? You gonna churn out a whole movie in two weeks? Mistake.

RAMEN
I'm halfway done already!

DAVE
(shrugs)
Good for you. Then what?

RAMEN

Then, I sell it and say goodbye to this Shipwreck forever!

DAVE

(smirks)

We all have dreams.

RAMEN

Like that, huh? What are your dreams?

DAVE

This is my dream, Ray. You know? "A working class hero is something to be."

RAMEN

Lennon!

DAVE

Familiar?

RAMEN

Mackie plays it on guitar.

DAVE

Mackie knows his shit!

RAMEN

I'm a working class hero, too.

DAVE

––No, you're more like "The Working Man,"
by Rush.

RAMEN

What does that mean?

DAVE

You think there's a better life out there . . . I
believe that's a lie.

RAMEN

(scoffs)
Rush played music for a living, dude. You
don't think that's a better life than this?

DAVE

At the end of the day it's still a job.

RAMEN

What's your problem tonight?

DAVE

I-I'm worried about you. Your head's in the
clouds.

RAMEN

Writing is a job to me, okay? It's what I'll do
for work.

DAVE

For the rest of your life?

RAMEN

Hope so!
(frustrated)
If you don't see that eventually I'll make
money from it, then you don't get it.

DAVE

No. I get it, Ray. The thing that worries me
is not that you might sell a movie script. In
fact, I really hope you do. It's awesome . . .
But there's too much money in movies. I'm

afraid that this movie thing isn't really your
dream. That you've been sold something by
Hollywood.

RAMEN
(sarcastically)
Oh, you're afraid? For me?

DAVE
Buddy, what if you wind up selling a movie
for a pile of cash? They move you out to Los
Angeles next. You're like 22, right?

Ramen nods.

And you have looks! Man, I've been around
the sun a few times. I've seen this play out.
It doesn't usually go well . . . You don't think
you're gonna get arrogant? --You're a ripe
enfant terrible.

RAMEN
What's an enfant terrible?

DAVE
Ask your girlfriend. It's French.

RAMEN
Wait, I don't understand. Are we not supposed to pursue our dreams? It's all I have,
man, this dream. You want to take that from
me, like my dad?

DAVE
Football was your dad's dream. I have a
question, Ray. Why didn't you take the football scholarship? You wouldn't have had to

work here . . . You could've still majored in
English and made your dad happy.

RAMEN

Simple. I was tired of getting the shit kicked
out of me.

DAVE

That's my point. Everyone gets the shit
kicked out of them in some way, shape, or
form. You--do it to yourself.

Ray scoffs and turns to the sink to wash glasses.

*The noisy intro of "Wishful Thinking" by Wilco begins to play softly
on the jukebox, and the song continues throughout the scene.*

After a brief moment, Dave places a hand on Ray's shoulder:

I'm sorry, bro. But it's true that money doesn't
buy happiness, mark my words. I want you
to be happy.

*The door opens and a slim ELDERLY MAN with short grey hair
walks toward the bar.*

RAMEN
(to elderly man)
How are you?

ELDERLY MAN
(in a foreign accent)
Be a whole lot better after a drink. Beer,
please.

*Ramen pours the man a beer. Dave continues reading behind the bar
next to Ramen.*

RAMEN
One beer for you sir. Where you from?

ELDERLY MAN
I'm a citizen of the world. I was born in Eastern Europe. I travel all over though, for work.

RAMEN
That sounds pretty neat.

ELDERLY MAN
(smiles)
My wife generally stays at our home in Vancouver.

RAMEN
Vancouver. I see. What do you do?

ELDERLY MAN
Consulting, mostly. I worked as a writer.
(a beat)
News, advertising . . . It's been a good life. Actually, this is my first time here in New Orleans.

Dave lowers Moby-Dick to chime in:

DAVE
(to the elderly man)
My friend Ramen here's an aspiring writer.

ELDERLY MAN
Wonderful!
(to Ramen)
What type of writing?

                    RAMEN
Screenwriting.

The man smiles.

                    ELDERLY MAN
Movies?

                    RAMEN
I'm trying to break in.

                    ELDERLY MAN
Good luck to you, son. That's a tricky business.

                    RAMEN
How so?

                    ELDERLY MAN
I've heard that it becomes hard to navigate at some point. A lot of money involved. Power politics. In other words, it's not as glorious as it might seem now.

The man looks around the barroom.

Honestly, this looks like a much happier life.

Ramen looks at Dave.

Dave shrugs.

                    DAVE
                  (to elderly man)
I'm trying to tell him! He's got a head like a brick.

INT./EXT. JEEP RIDE – NIGHT

Ramen drives his Jeep through the streets of New Orleans toward the French Quarter, wearing a white, collared work shirt and khaki shorts.

"Voodoo Child" by Jimi Hendrix plays on the radio.

He's smoking a joint.

INSERT – DATE
Friday, April 20, 2007

SUDDENLY he notices Sheila sitting next to him in the passenger seat, wearing a crop top T-shirt bearing the name of the band Voodoo Glow Skulls.

>   RAMEN
>   *(smirks)*
>   If I'm not writing, I don't need you.

She smiles.

>   SHEILA
>   *(softly)*
>   Where are you going?

>   RAMEN
>   A voodoo ritual . . .

>   SHEILA
>   What if you see something you don't like?

>   RAMEN
>   Chance I'm willing to take.

>   SHEILA
>   You're in danger, Ray.

RAMEN
(*scoffs*)
Nonsense. You're a voice in my head, remember? I'm doing exactly what I want.

SHEILA
Maybe that's the problem. You always do what you want. Maybe your friends have been trying to tell you something.

RAMEN
Everyone's always trying to tell me something, all at once . . . Go away!

SHEILA
"As you wish."

When he glances at her, for a moment she looks like JILL.

––Talk to Jill lately?

He tries to speak, but no one's there.

INT./EXT. VOODOO GIFT SHOP – NIGHT

Ramen paces back and forth in front of the voodoo shop, nervously, smoking a cigarette. He looks in the window and sees Jacques standing ALONE inside the shop by the register. He's wearing all black and his signature fedora, writing in a ledger. He notices Ray and waves at him. Then, Jacques stores the ledger in a drawer, turns out the lights, and walks outside to greet Ramen with a smile.

JACQUES
Good evening, Ramen.

RAMEN
Evening.

Jacques faces the door to lock up the shop.

> JACQUES
> You look nervous. You sure you want to come with me?

> RAMEN
> *(a little defensive)*
> I'm fine.

> JACQUES
> Okay . . . First, I have to blindfold you.

> RAMEN
> What?

> JACQUES
> I'm kidding! We just have to walk a few blocks.

Ramen laughs uncomfortably.

FRENCH QUARTER STREETS – CONTINUOUS

Ramen and Jacques proceed to walk together toward the site of the ritual. After they turn from the commercial street, it gets quieter and more devoid of anyone else walking by.

> RAMEN
> Should I know anything specific before going into this?

> JACQUES
> I have a few tips for you. One, just try to have an open mind. Have your questions ready to be answered beforehand, and it will work out for you. Think directly as possible.

RAMEN
Okay, open mind. Questions ready . . .

JACQUES
Two, remember that you are surrounded at all times by the spirits of both your ancestors, and many, many loas.

RAMEN
Wait, what are loas?

JACQUES
Loas are voodoo gods. Spirits that have come into being through thousands of years of experience and practice by others.
(a beat)
Some are nicer than others.

RAMEN
Are some of them mean?

JACQUES
Harsh might be a better word. Focus on the good.

ARMSTRONG PARK, TREME – CONTINUOUS

They enter Armstrong Park and pass a STATUE of Louis Armstrong.

A local band plays none other than "Heebie Jeebies" by Louis Armstrong on stage in front of a small audience.

Ramen recognizes the song and shudders.

JACQUES
Something wrong?

RAMEN
It's weird. That song plays in my dreams.

JACQUES
Maybe your mind is already open.

RAMEN
To what, coincidence?

JACQUES
If that's what you call it. I like synchronicity.

Ramen shrugs.

RAMEN
What's that?

JACQUES
A meaningful coincidence.

They exit the park, and the music fades.

TREME NEIGHBORHOOD STREET – CONTINUOUS

They traverse a quiet residential street.

They reach an old house with overgrown foliage.

JACQUES
This is it.

RAMEN
This looks like someone's house, maybe?

JACQUES
Follow me. This way to the backyard.

RAMEN
It's in somebody's backyard?

Jacques nods.

They walk up a dark, narrow passageway along the old house. The famous musician Dr. John passes them in the alley going the other way.

> *(to Jacques; quietly)*
> You know who that was!

> JACQUES
> You may see familiar faces, Ramen. Keep it
> to yourself.

Ray nods.

BACKYARD – CONTINUOUS

They approach a large SHED in the backyard of the house and reach the door.

> JACQUES
> One last thing, Ramen . . . if you are mount-
> ed by a spirit tonight––

SUDDENLY, LOUISE, a charismatic BLACK WOMAN with an Afro hairstyle, dressed in a sheer, sleeveless GOWN with a sequined SASH around her waist opens the door and interrupts them.

> LOUISE
> Hey, Jacques, you get more handsome every
> time I see you!

He warmly kisses her on the cheek.

> JACQUES
> You're not so bad yourself!

She wags her finger at him.

> LOUISE
> You keep flirting with me, Jacques! Some-

thing's gonna happen!

> JACQUES
> You started it!

She chuckles.

> LOUISE
> Oh, good! You brought your friend.
> *(to Ray)*
> I'm Priestess Louise, honey. This is my home. Make yourself comfortable.

She holds out her hand to greet him, and they shake hands.

> RAMEN
> Ramen Noodle.

> LOUISE
> Pleasure to meet you! Come on in!

She opens the door, and Ramen walks in.

Louise turns to Jacques at the doorway:

> *(aside; mouthing)*
> Ramen Noodle?

Jacques shrugs.

They enter.

INT. BACKYARD VOODOO TEMPLE – NIGHT

The TEMPLE: a single, open room lacking in flair, dimly lit by CANDLELIGHT and cigarettes. Twenty or so people, mostly black and creole, sit in FOLDING CHAIRS around the ALTAR in two rows.

In front of the altar: a proportional STAGE, raised about a foot off the ground. It bears a LARGE PAINTING of the heart and dagger veve symbol.

A group of three men are playing a steady beat on bongo-like Haitian DRUMS to one side of the altar.

On the other side of the altar are two live chickens in a cage.

Heavy INCENSE burns in a DISH atop the altar, which also features a bottle of dark RUM and a carafe of red WINE.

Ramen notices a wide age-range of people but no children. The men in the audience wear loose-fitting SHIRTS and pants in a variety of colors, leather sandals, BOOTS.

One man wears a TOP HAT and smokes a cigar. His face, painted, resembles a skull. He eyes Ramen with a grin. Is this really a man?

Women wear bold JEWELRY (some featuring BONES), their dresses range from homely to utterly provocative, sheer GOWNS.

The congregation acts contently—softly speaking to one another, some laughing, some smoking. Others appearing meditative and solemn.

Louise ushers Ramen and Jacques to their seats along a sidewall, and the two men sit.

RAMEN
(to Louise)

Thanks.

LOUISE

Be blessed, honey. Bless you too, Jacques.

JACQUES

Appreciate you, Louise.

Louise winks at Jacques. Then, she waves to someone before taking a seat next to the stage.

RAMEN
(to Jacques; whispers)
Were you trying to tell me something?

JACQUES
(quietly)
Yes . . . if you are mounted by a spirit tonight,
do not be afraid. Voodoo is trying to——

He's interrupted by a drumming crescendo. Everyone stands. The drumming stops.

RAMEN

    To what?

JACQUES

    To reach you.

The door opens and in walks an OUNGAN, the voodoo priest. A short, thick, dark-skinned man of 60. He's barefoot and shirtless, wearing baggy linen pants and a red silk sash around his waste. This is complimented by a fresh cowboy hat made of straw.

He's holding a box under his arm like the wooden box from Ramen's dream. But it isn't glowing.

RAMEN
(to Jacques)

    The priest?

JACQUES
(whispers)

    Oungan, in voodoo.

RAMEN
What's in the box?

JACQUES
(kidding)
Severed head, maybe.

The drum beat picks up tempo.

Ramen notices a familiar face standing across the room from him. It's JUDAS, in a red, hooded robe, STARING AT HIM.

Ray goes white with fear.

RAMEN
(whispers)
The alligator man is here . . .

JACQUES
(dismissively)
Try to pay attention.

The oungan dances randomly, if not convulsively to the drumming, at the same time walking toward the altar.

Others in the audience begin to sway freely, moving their hips and arms to the beat.

The drumming stops when the oungan reaches the stage.

He places the box on the altar and opens it. INSIDE: an alligator HATCHLING.

The oungan turns back toward the CONGREGATION holding the reptile in front of him. He addresses them:

OUNGAN
(energetically)
Welcome, everyone! Good evening children

of Marie Laveau . . . Welcome Legba, Samedi, Ezili . . . our ancestors, spirits, loas. Tonight we are honored to worship together, acknowledging your ever-guiding presence.

CONGREGATION
Welcome oungan!

OUNGAN
Manbo Louise, would you join me on stage to invoke the loa.

Louise joins him on the raised platform.

CONGREGATION
Praise manbo!

Louise, smiling, gestures graciously to the congregation.

OUNGAN
Music please. It's time to channel the spirits.

The drummers begin with a steady MARCHING BEAT.

Louise closes her eyes and begins to move her hips. She raises her arms above her head and dances seductively.

The oungan sets the alligator on the altar. Then, he begins dancing with Louise. Intently focused on her midsection but without actual contact, he holds his hands out near her hips as they go. Moving down and up, he squats and rises in front of her and dances as though she has a minor forcefield around her.

JACQUES
(quietly; to Ray)
A fertility prayer.

Ramen remains distracted by JUDAS and doesn't respond.

The drum beat picks up, and the crowd sways and gesticulates, some rhythmically and some more awkwardly.

A SECOND MAN from the crowd feels compelled to join the oungan and Louise on stage. He begins dancing behind her with his arms in the air like an unseen transfer of power, eyes focused on her movements, not disturbing either of them in the least.

Ramen begins to move his shoulders like he's beginning to dance—or lose control. He looks at Jacques whose moving in a deeper meditative state with his EYES CLOSED.

OUNGAN
(shouting)

Open your ears . . . Listen everyone to their wisdom! Hear them speaking to you!

Ramen sways back and forth. He tilts his head, bewildered once more at the sight of Judas glaring at him from across the room.

Open your minds! Let them into your souls!

SUDDENLY Ramen's eyes roll to the back of his head . . .

EXT. COSMIC BEACH REALM – NIGHT (A DREAM)

Ramen finds himself alone in a dreamy cosmic space, somewhat familiar but also unlike anything he's ever seen. It resembles the SHORE of a deserted ISLAND under millions of STARS and comets. The drum beat fades to the sound of PALM TREES swaying in the breeze and crystal blue water breaking softly on the shore. The SAND is grey, and it sparkles under light from a gigantic MOON above.

He walks a few paces, looking around and taking it all in.

He reaches down and takes a handful of glittering sand. He lets it fall through his fingers.

                    RAMEN'S VOICE
                      (thinking)
This is beautiful!

*SUDDENLY he notices a figure standing in a BLOOD RED ROBE
and an ALLIGATOR MASK. It's Judas, completely still and facing
him up ahead, holding a familiar, glowing box.*

                        JUDAS
                      (chillingly)
Why are you here?

                        RAMEN
                      (confused)
I don't know . . . Where are we, Haiti?

                        JUDAS
No. A spirit island. You've been mounted by
a loa. Speak up!

                        RAMEN
Okay . . . Who are you?

                        JUDAS
I am Judas. This contains the spirit of your
obsession.

                        RAMEN
                     (indignantly)
Obsession?

                        JUDAS
You may become anything you want, Ramen. But at a cost.

The eyes of the alligator man begin to glow reddish, and the box glows brighter. Ramen takes a small step backward.

RAMEN

What? I don't understand.

JUDAS

Do you know what sacrifice means?

RAMEN

Like in my dreams?

JUDAS

Yes.

RAMEN

Wait! Are you going to kill me?

JUDAS

Your ambition will be your undoing. I'm here to warn you.

RAMEN

So . . . don't write my movie?

JUDAS

If you continue on your path, you will be sacrificed. It's your choice . . .

RAMEN
(a beat)

What a joke, man! I'm at this stupid voodoo ritual looking for help, and who do I run into? You! Huge fucking joke!
(trembling)
Why don't you stay out of my head, creepy-ass psycho! Writing a movie is all I care about! That's my choice!

JUDAS

This is not a joke.

Thunderous, gray clouds form up above. Ray continues to rant, but he's made a decision.

RAMEN
(shouting)

Tell you what, gator guy! I'll die if I don't write this movie! So, why don't you un-mount me, or do whatever the hell it is you have to do to get me away from here—

The Alligator Man, in a frightening instant, appears directly in front of Ray. After a brief moment, he draws the dagger and slices Ray's throat with it. Ramen grips at his mortal wound in a state of shock, and then falls lifelessly to the ground.

The monster crouches on all fours, approaches slowly, and eats, ending the dream.

BACK TO:

INT. BACKYARD VOODOO TEMPLE – NIGHT

Ramen comes to, standing. He grips his throat. It's not cut. Then, he takes a deep breath, hugging himself before calming down.

He's now in the midst of the voodoo ritual having grown in intensity. Everyone's dancing together or in their own world, including Jacques. Rum and wine are being passed around the congregation. The little alligator is still on the altar. A CHICKEN has been slaughtered at the neck, with blood on the stage.

SUDDENLY Judas appears next to him, without the mask. Ramen is startled. Judas hands him the dagger.

JUDAS

Take it.

Ramen accepts the gift and darts toward the door clumsily, bumping into people on the way out.

INT./EXT. JEEP RIDE – NIGHT – CONTINUOUS

Ramen turns on the Jeep radio, and the tune of "Just" by Radiohead plays—"You do it to yourself, you do, and that's what really hurts." It plays as he drives away from the French Quarter, smoking a cigarette, passing familiar places.

                                        FADE TO BLACK:

INT. THE SHIPWRECK BAR – NIGHT

"In Love With You" by Erykah Badu plays softly on the jukebox.

RAIN falls heavily outside. Jill towel-dries bar glasses by hand. Dave sits at the bar with a pint, facing Jill.

His copy of Moby-Dick is on the bar.

INSERT – DATE

Wednesday, April 25, 2007

> JILL
> Ray would be disappointed at this, but what
> is Moby-Dick about, exactly? A whale?

> DAVE
> It's a tell-tale about what happens when our
> ambition goes off the rails.

> JILL
> ––What happens?

> DAVE
> I'm pretty sure everyone's gonna die.

Jill leans on the bar across from Dave. She frowns.

> Why the long face? How's Ray?

> JILL
> Ugh. He's spending all of his time writing. He's got a big meeting with producers next week.

> DAVE
> Oh, that's right!

Jill pours a soda. She takes a sip.

> JILL
> This is the fourth shift I've covered for him in a row ... I feel neglected!

> DAVE
> Jill ...

> JILL
> Dave.

> DAVE
> Look, I know you really like Ray. I think he likes you too, but ...

> JILL
> What are you trying to say?

> DAVE
> I don't know. Forget it.

> JILL
> *(sighs; quietly)*
> I just need him to get his act together.

INT. RAMEN'S BEDROOM – NIGHT

*Ramen sits at the computer in front of his script with a bottle of ab-
sinthe, wearing a T-shirt bearing Einstein's face that reads, "The ab-
sinthe-minded professor."*

INSERT – DATE

Friday, April 27, 2007

*Sheila lies at the foot of his bed in alluring pajamas. Ray notices her
attractiveness momentarily.*

> RAMEN
>
> Glad you're here! I have a meeting with ex-
> ecs from Everest on Thursday. They want
> two days in advance to review the script.
> That means you're gonna help me wrap this
> up by Monday.

> SHEILA
>
> Ramen, how's Jill?

> RAMEN
>
> An imaginary friend questioning their cre-
> ator . . . Now I know how God feels.

> SHEILA
>
> You're being unfair to her.

> RAMEN
>
> You know what's unfair? This deadline is
> unfair! Focus, okay!

Sheila blows some hair off of her face.

> ––How did you provoke this monster? Do
> you deserve to die?

SHEILA

I didn't do anything! He's possessed––He
wants to eat me!

RAMEN

He ate me, and I'm still here. Where were
you during that whole ordeal?

SHEILA

You're the hero, remember?

*He pours the last, green bit of absinthe over a sugar cube, lights it on
fire, adds water, and stirs it in with the spoon.*

You're not supposed to light it on fire.

RAMEN

Fun though!

*He gazes into the liquor glass for a moment. Then he looks at the DAG-
GER that Judas gave him, sitting on the desk.*

SHEILA

... We should take a survey from your neigh-
bors.

RAMEN
                (to himself, slurred)
A vision of collision with division is a decision.

SHEILA

Maybe stop with the absinthe. You have a
screenplay to complete. Can we get back to
the point?

RAMEN
Maybe there is no point . . .

He looks at her lying on his bed.

Only instinct.

SHEILA
Don't look at me like that! I'm not real!

He turns back toward the computer screen.

RAMEN
(snappy)
Just tell me what to write, then!

SHEILA
Fine. Got your typing fingers ready?

He gives her a sharp look.

The Alligator Man has my whole parish fooled. He's a priest, but in secret he's practicing an outlaw brand of voodoo with a penchant for revenge against descendants of French colonists, such as yours truly and my boyfriend, Randy . . .

The words fade off.

INT./EXT. RAMEN'S BEDROOM – MORNING

Jill stands outside, knocking determinedly on Ramen's door.

Hungover, Ray awakens with some difficulty. He immediately scans the bed for Sheila next to him, but she's not there.

SUDDENLY, the ALLIGATOR MAN stands at the foot of his bed, holding the dagger.

Ramen shudders. He wipes his eyes and looks again, only to see his bedroom.

INSERT – DATE

Monday, April 30, 2007

He rises and opens the door.

Jill enters, wearing a backpack. She's cradling a bottle of absinthe in her arms.

JILL

I brought you something.

He takes the bottle from her and places it on his desk. He SLIDES the dagger on his desk underneath a stack of paper.

RAMEN

You're so thoughtful! I ran out.

JILL
(shrugs)

I guess . . . Get dressed sexy man, you're walking me to class for making me work for you all last week.

RAMEN

You're a superstar. How was it?

JILL

Comme ci, comme ça. It rained a bunch. I actually just sat there with Dave most of the time.

RAMEN
(winces; jestingly)

Y'all bonded?

JILL
At least I know he loves the Beastie Boys.

RAMEN
You may never have known that otherwise.

Jill shoots him a look.

JILL
I hope you're getting some work done, Mr. Mankiewicz.

RAMEN
Citizen Kane!

Jill nods.

. . . I'm done--just about. It's drafted, anyway. I have to bring it to them this afternoon so they can review it for Thursday.

JILL
Mon Dieu! How's that feel?

RAMEN
I don't even know! What if they hate it and cancel the meeting?

JILL
Ray, look at me.

She has his attention.

You're going to crush it.

Ramen sighs.

RAMEN
I hope you're right.

JILL
I'm right. Now c'mon, I don't want to be late!

She heads outside.

Ramen hurries to get dressed but stops for a moment to look around the room.

RAMEN
(whispers)
Sheila?

She doesn't answer.

EXT. LAKE PONTCHARTRAIN LEVEE TRAIL – DAY

Ramen and Jill walk along Lake Pontchartrain on the levee trail toward campus.

Jill stops him in his tracks. She gets in front of him.

JILL
Hey, where have you been, Ramen?

RAMEN
What? My apartment.

JILL
I mean, where is your head?

RAMEN
(stumped)
... I guess your right. Maybe I've been a little absinthe.

JILL

Absinthe?

RAMEN
(*grimaces*)
––Absent! Is what I meant to say!

He smiles. Jill does not.

JILL

I'm not kidding! We haven't really talked since our date.

He loses the grin.

RAMEN

Jill, I'm here with you, right now . . . Look, I know I'm wrapped up with this screenplay deal, but I'm just excited because I finally have a shot.

JILL

A shot at what, exactly?

RAMEN

C'mon! Making a name for myself! Establishing myself as an actual screenwriter. Not just some college kid bartender!

JILL

You must really think the world of me, then!

RAMEN

That's not what I meant. I want you to know that ever since the first time I saw you my luck's been changing. We hit it off . . . and I actually wrote a movie––

Jill gives a patronizing smile.

What's that smile?

JILL
. . . Movie, movie, movie! Do you care about me?

RAMEN
Of course I do! I know I've been a little distant. But everything's going to change this week.

JILL
I understand, but to me you're great, either way. That's all! I never expected to find you. I'm happy about the way things are going for you, but I'm in love with you. I needed to hear you say that I matter to you, too.

They hug and kiss affectionately.

You owe me dinner, and a movie.

Ramen smiles.

I mean it! And I'm not picking up anymore shifts for you! I have school, too, and finals!

He kisses her again.

RAMEN
Dinner, then! Tomorrow!

JILL
(coyly)
I'll check my schedule.

He laughs.

INT. COLLEGE CLASSROOM – DAY

Professor Green stands at the podium in front of a dark classroom.

The class watches a screening of A Clockwork Orange.

Ramen and MELODY sit in the back of the classroom, as usual.

> RAMEN
> *(quietly; to Melody)*
> Hey, I'm leaving. I have to go drop some-
> thing off today.

> MELODY
> *(whispers)*
> Green's not gonna like that.

Ray shrugs.

> RAMEN
> *(quietly)*
> He'll get over it. I've seen this more than
> once.

He gets up and walks out.

Green looks perturbed, but doesn't speak.

INT. CONFERENCE ROOM – MORNING

Ray's big meeting with Everest Films. He sits at a polished wooden conference table, dressed in a shirt and tie. In front of him on the table lies a cup of COFFEE, and his printed SCRIPT, titled "HOLY EVIL."

INSERT – DATE

Thursday, May 3, 2007

Across from Ramen, three PRODUCER-types are seated:

PRODUCER #1 sits on Ramen's left. He is a middle-aged man, over-weight, with a balding mullet hairdo, likely been awake all night, wearing a bright-colored tropical print shirt.

PRODUCER #2 sits in the middle of the three, has a more conservative appearance. Yet, she seems oddly distracted, looking around the room at intervals. She's also elderly, with wrinkled features, wearing a designer suit.

PRODUCER #3 sits on Ramen's right, an annoyingly condescending, young rich guy go-getter, also wearing a fancy suit, has a slick hairdo. Muscular and a well-defined jawline, he wears pretentious glasses.

COFFEE MUGS sit in front of each studio executive. In front of PRO-DUCER #2 lies a leather PORTFOLIO and a gold PEN.

Producer #1 and Producer #3 look at each other to decide who will begin, kind of ignoring Producer #2. Producer #2 begins:

PRODUCER #2

We adore your story, Ramen. Just adore it.
I——

PRODUCER #1
(interrupts)

We totally dig your screenplay, Ramen. Alligator Man? I was like, duh! Why didn't I think of that!

PRODUCER #3
(clears throat)

Considering your age and education, exceptional, Ramen. We'd like to offer you a three-movie deal out of this.

RAMEN
Wait, what! Like a trilogy!

PRODUCER #1
(*smiles*)
Like a trilogy, Ramen.

Ramen sits up straight.

RAMEN
Hold up. Is this a dream?

PRODUCER #3
(*smiles*)
More like a dream come true, Ramen.

PRODUCER #1
(*interrupts*)
I, for one, feel like this movie could potentially be "the one" next Halloween. It's got everything: mystery, demons, sex––

PRODUCER #2
(*interrupts*)
Not to mention, a handsome, young writer––

PRODUCER #3
Right. We want three movies out of this script, Ramen. So, the way we see it you're just getting started.

RAMEN
Awesome! Where do I sign?

PRODUCER #1
Just a second, Ramen. This is all bound by a

contract, of course. Can I be frank?

RAMEN

Sure!

PRODUCER #1

You're a young writer––

RAMEN

Not that young . . .

Producer #2 smiles.

PRODUCER #1

Eh, listen, you're twenty-two . . . That's young in my book, especially to hit a home run! Young people in this business––young, successful people like you, tend to fade out––

PRODUCER #3
(interrupts)

––This isn't baseball that we're playing. I think what my friend is trying to say is that as you know by now, Ray, writing is hard work.

RAMEN

I keep telling my friend Dave––

PRODUCER #1
(interrupts)

We just hope you're not too easily distracted is what I think we're all saying.

Producer #2 sits calmly, her eyes blankly scanning the room. Producers #1 and #3 ignore her, turn to one another, and nod in agreement over what was just said.

*An intern, WILL, enters the conference room with a coffee pot. He
refills for Producer #1.*

Keep it coming, please, Will.

WILL
Yes, sir.

*Producer #2 ignores the intern, and #1 waves off the offering. He comes
around to Ray.*

More coffee, Mr. Noodle?

RAMEN
No, thanks.

Will exits the room.

PRODUCER #3
That's William. He writes, too.

PRODUCER #2
Does he?

PRODUCER #3
He does.
(to Ramen)
He's about your age though . . . Thousands
of guys like him literally want to be you right
now, Ray. Do you understand that?

RAMEN
Think I'm picking up what you're putting
down.

PRODUCER #3
One day you're up, and the next day you're
down in Hollywood. It's the nature of the
business!

                            RAMEN
Did you say Hollywood?

                          PRODUCER #3
Yes.

                            RAMEN
                           (a beat)
Do I have to move to Hollywood?

The producers look at each other apprehensively.

                          PRODUCER #1
Well, yeah, Ramen. We can help you find a
place to your liking--

                            RAMEN
Most of the movie is set in Louisiana.

                          PRODUCER #1
That doesn't mean we're going to film it all
here. We'll probably film most of it at the
studio in Los Angeles.

                          PRODUCER #3
That's right, Ray. And we already have rough
outlines worked out for the trilogy that may
not involve Louisiana much at all . . . Is that
going to be a problem?

Producer #2 pushes the portfolio across the table to Ramen. He scans:

INSERT – CONTRACT

*". . . Writer will be bound by Everest Films to complete two more
screenplays, on schedule, deadlines determined by Everest Films."*

Ramen shrugs, then scans further:

CONTRACT

"If at any point the studio deems it necessary that one or more additional writers assist with the project, Everest Films bears the sole right to make that decision if and when the time comes.

"Any and all work in the form of screenplay by writer will automatically be property of Everest Films until contract expires in 2014."

His face tightens. He scans further:

CONTRACT

"Everest Films agrees to pay writer $350,000 in a single installment immediately upon signing. And again upon completion of each subsequent screenplay for horror movie trilogy, 'Holy Evil.'"

Producer #2 holds out the gold pen for him.

PRODUCER #2

Here you go, darling.

Ramen looks at Producer #2 and scans the eager faces of the other two. He takes a deep breath.

RAMEN

Ugh! I can't do it.

PRODUCER #3

Is something wrong with our offer, Ramen?
We can go back over it, but we deem this
quite generous for your first movie.
(to Producer #1)
What's his face didn't get that good of an offer—

PRODUCER #1

There's plenty to do in Los Angeles, man!
Have you ever surfed before?

                              RAMEN
No . . . Guys, the offer's fine! I just can't. I'm
sorry. If it's as good as you say it is, maybe I
need to weigh all my options––

                         PRODUCER #2
Take all the time you nee––

                              RAMEN
    Kidding!

He laughs.

The producers all begin to laugh uneasily with him.

This is everything I've ever dreamed of! I
promise I won't let y'all down! Holy shit!
Thanks, so much!

                         PRODUCER #2
    He's adorable . . .

INT./EXT. JILL'S BEDROOM – EVENING

*Ramen stands outside Jill's apartment, holding a large BOUQUET of
flowers.*

He breathes, and then knocks on the door.

*Jill opens the door, wearing GLASSES and sweatpants. She gazes at
Ramen for a moment, and smiles.*

                              JILL
    For me?

He nods.

RAMEN
I sold my script.

JILL
Oh, mon Dieu! Are you fucking serious?

RAMEN
As a heart attack.

Jill screams excitedly. She tosses the flowers on her bed and jumps on Ramen, wrapping her arms and legs around him.

He carries her inside. They fall to the bed, Jill on top.

JILL
I think we smashed the flowers!

He shrugs. They laugh.

RAMEN
I'll get you some more.

JILL
I'm so proud of you! Asshole!

They kiss, happily.

RAMEN
I made it, Jill.

JILL
You made it--wait, are you rich?

RAMEN
You have no idea.

JILL
Oh my God, is your mom excited?

RAMEN
(laughs)
Is she! She won't stop about the LEGO's!

JILL
I need to meet this woman ... Wait, LEGO's?

RAMEN
It's how you put a screenplay together ...
piece by piece.

JILL
Hm. You know how to put a relationship together?

RAMEN
How?

JILL
Kiss by kiss.

They kiss again.

INT. COLLEGE CLASSROOM – DAY

Professor Green stands behind a podium in front of the class.

INSERT – DATE

Monday, May 7, 2007 (Less than two weeks 'til graduation)

Ramen's desk is empty.

PROFESSOR GREEN
Does anyone happen to know where Ramen
Noodle has been . . . Death in the family?
Disease, maybe?

No one speaks. MELODY raises a hand. Green points to her.

                    MELODY
I can fill him in.

                  PROFESSOR GREEN
Okay . . .

He smiles.

    It's the last week of class. I mean, everyone
    else bothered to be here . . .

He shakes his head and sighs.

    Alright, let's pick up from yesterday. Anyone
    remember?

                    STUDENT
I thought we started talking about the Indi-
ana Jones movies.

                  PROFESSOR GREEN
We did, perfect! Let's see, "Raiders of the
Lost Ark" is pivotal to modern film. Can
anyone say why?

                   SARA BISHOP
Timing!

*Ramen enters the classroom and stands by the door. His T-shirt reads
"Wait and Hope" (a Count of Monte Cristo reference).*

                  PROFESSOR GREEN
Ramen, quit disturbing the class and take a
chair!

                    RAMEN
I'm fine right here.

Professor Green walks from the podium over to Ramen and gets in his face.

He points to Ray's desk.

> PROFESSOR GREEN
> (quietly)
> Do I have to draw you a map?

Ray stares back at him.

> Let's go have a word in the hallway.

INT. UNIVERSITY BUILDING HALLWAY – CONTINUOUS

The hallway is empty and silent. Professor Green steps out of the classroom just before Ramen and shuts the door behind them.

CLASSROOM – CONTINUOUS

The whole class pops up from their seats and gathers against the door to listen.

> BACK TO:

UNIVERSITY BUILDING HALLWAY

Ramen and Green face one another.

> PROFESSOR GREEN
> You mind explaining to me, "A" why your attendance has been dismal the past two weeks, and "B" why you're being a pain in the ass?

> RAMEN
> (scoffs)
> Spare me . . .

PROFESSOR GREEN

You're barely treading water, son. I'd choose my next words wisely if I were you.

RAMEN
(quietly)

I sold a screenplay.

PROFESSOR GREEN

You what?

RAMEN

Everest Films offered me three-hundred and fifty thousand for my horror screenplay . . . They want a trilogy.

Green scratches his chin.

PROFESSOR GREEN

Well, I'll be jitterbugged! I don't know what to say, Ramen. Good for you, man . . . You want to go inside and preach the good news?

RAMEN
(beat)

I won't give you the satisfaction, prick.

PROFESSOR GREEN

What did you say?

RAMEN
(with force)

I said: You're a prick!

Professor Green drops Ray to the floor with one, solid fist.

Ramen lies flat on his back, with a BLOODY NOSE, looking up at Green.

Green crouches down over him.

RAMEN
Ouch! You sucker punched me!

PROFESSOR GREEN
I'm sorry, Ramen. You're a big boy. I didn't
know if you were gonna hit me first.

*Professor Green offers to pull Ray back on his feet, but Ray yanks him
toward the ground and they start to tussle on the ground. Green eventually renders him motionless.*

Are you finished!

RAMEN
(struggling)
I pity you.

PROFESSOR GREEN
Watch it!

The classroom door opens, spilling the whole class into the hallway.

*Ramen's classmates AD LIB reactions to the scene: looking around at
one another, wincing, and covering their mouths in awe.*

Among them, stands MELODY.

Green lets him loose and they both get back to their feet.

*Ramen sways, holding his nose with both hands. He finds his balance
and steps closer to Green.*

RAMEN
(to Green)
I haven't said my piece.

PROFESSOR GREEN
(shrugs)
The gang's all here.

RAMEN
Why don't you get off of your high horse and
actually help someone?

PROFESSOR GREEN
(smirks)
What do you think I've done with you?

RAMEN
(loudly)
Stop fucking with our heads, man! All anyone can think about after your class is money! You've got every last one of us so far off
base about writing that it makes me sick!

Ramen spits blood on the floor, then wipes his mouth.

PROFESSOR GREEN
You sure that's not all the booze and pot
talking, Ramen?

Ray gives him a sharp look.

What, you don't think everyone knows who
you are by now?

RAMEN
(smirks; to classmates)
Without the writers there'd be no film industry. It's an art form. It comes from the
heart. It takes sacrifice, dreams . . . love. But
the industry, even at the school level, seems
concerned with one thing: money. If you

want to become a screenwriter, you're pressured into outrageous tuitions––what for? So someone like him can glorify the haves and tell you that you have no real friends?

PROFESSOR GREEN
You can't handle reality, son!

RAMEN
(to class)
None of you are up against anything but yourselves . . . If you have something to say, y'all, start writing! Don't let anyone distract you with their lies.

Ramen takes a deep breath and moves a couple steps backwards.

He wipes the blood from his mouth.

His classmates exchange looks at one another and whispers.

Professor Green begins to clap.

PROFESSOR GREEN
Bravo, Che Guevara . . . That was a heartfelt monologue, if I've ever heard one. But wait, does the class know about how you just sold out to Everest Films for your horror movie?

The class looks confused.

(to class)
That's right. The altruist here only graced us with his presence today for one reason: to gloat.

MELODY takes a step forward.

MELODY

You sold a script, Ray?

He nods.

RAMEN

Everest offered me three-hundred and fifty thousand for a horror I wrote.

MELODY

What? Holy shit! Is this real life?

RAMEN

They want me to write two more.

MELODY
(smiles; to classmates)

––Let's all go to The Shipwreck and buy Ray a beer! He's good for it! Three cheers for Ray, y'all! Hip hip hooray!

DOUG
(chiming)

Hip hip hooray!

ENTIRE CLASS
(together)

Hip hip hooray! Hip hip hooray! Hip hip hooray! Ray! Ray! Ray! Ray! Ray!

Ray's classmates swarm close to him in admiration and cheerfulness. Two STRONG CLASSMATES pick him up on their shoulders in the middle of the pack. Even Green can't withhold a grin.

(together)

Noodle! Noodle! Noodle!

They exit down the hall, chanting while Green scratches his head.

INT. THE SHIPWRECK BAR – EVENING

The ENTIRE CLASS, gathered in pockets, except for Green, party at THE SHIPWRECK, celebrating Ray's success with merriment and cheer.

Jill sits next to Ray in a booth, and they couldn't be happier.

Dave and Cousin Mackie work behind the bar, pouring drinks for the packed house and kidding around.

> DAVE
> *(to Mackie)*
> I finished reading Moby-Dick last night.

> MACKIE
> I think I saw the movie years ago. How was
> it?

> DAVE
> Really good . . . tragic.

> MACKIE
> That's what I remember.

TABLE

Sara Bishop sits across from two students.

> SARA BISHOP
> I mean, I'm happy for him . . . But get real,
> I'm way more talented!

One of her friends shrugs.

> Whatever . . . I can't wait to transfer to UCLA.

BOOTH

Melody sits across from Ray and Jill with drinks.

MELODY
(to Ramen)

I didn't know you had a girlfriend, Ray! How long has this been going on?

RAMEN

About a month––
(smiles; to Jill)
Huh, good lookin?

JILL
(to Melody)

Love at first sight.
(to Ray)
Je t'adore. Embrasse-moi.

They kiss.

MACKIE
(to Ramen; hollers)

You da man, stab-ah!

Ramen folds his hands toward Mackie in gratitude.

Doug Mills approaches their booth.

DOUG
(to Ray)

Are you going to sue Green?

RAMEN
(shrugs)

Probably not . . .

DOUG

I would.

RAMEN
It wasn't exactly unprovoked.

Jill touches his bruised face. Ray winces.

Please don't touch it!

JILL
He got you good, didn't he?

DOUG
––So, Ray, now that you've got an "in" with Everest, you think you might pass along my script to them?

RAMEN
Sure, I'll see what I can do!

Someone plays "Voodoo" by Godsmack on the jukebox, an eerie heavy metal song.

A large man in a blood-red, hooded robe enters the bar.

SLO-MO

He walks in through the crowd and lowers his hood . . . It's Judas. No one else appears to notice him. He approaches the bar to order a drink. After a moment, he turns his head and locks eyes with Ramen.

Ramen's face tightens and he turns white.

INT. HIGH-RISE CONDO, LOS ANGELES – DAY

Ramen sits alone on a sofa, staring listlessly at us. He's in a fancy, modern condominium in the downtown area.

ALLIGATOR MADE OF LEGO'S

Sits on an end table.

INSERT – DATE

Five Months Later

Upon further review, the place is a total mess.

Empty liquor and beer bottles, pizza boxes, and fast-food bags litter the countertop and floors . . . Holes in the walls, stains.

Cocaine and pot are spread out on the coffee table.

A lamp and a barstool are flipped over.

SHEILA lies asleep somewhere on the floor, her appearance disheveled.

A HANDWRITTEN letter from Jill sits next to Ray on the sofa.

INSERT – LETTER

"Ray, I've tried to be there for you . . . It's been weeks now and it's impossible to get a hold of you. I know you're working, I guess. But I'm not feeling appreciated, and life's too short to hold onto something that's not bringing you joy. You never even said you love me until recently, and I don't think you meant it. It sounded like you were at a party . . . I'm dating other people. I think it's best if you move on, too. XOXO, Au revoir, Jill."

INSERT – CELL PHONE

"Mom: 22 Missed Calls"

"Don't Stop Believin'" plays, and he reluctantly answers.

MOM'S VOICE

Ramen, oh my God, do I need to come get you?

RAMEN

Please don't.

MOM'S VOICE
Son, I have called you--I don't even want to say how many times. Is this about your father?

RAMEN
Don't.

MOM'S VOICE
Don't tell me don't! I talked to him. He said he's going out there to have a talk with you. He doesn't like the way things have been going. He's been stubborn. We're both worried about you!

RAMEN
(quietly)
Please stop calling so much.
(louder)
--I'll call you if I want to talk!

MOM'S VOICE
Fine, Ramen, have it your way! Your dad's on his way out th--

Ray hangs up on her, click. DIAL TONE...

A KNOCK on the door. He looks around. Sheila's gone.

RAMEN
(a beat)
Who's there?

It's quiet.

Ramen gets up and opens the door. It's the ALLIGATOR MAN. He's holding the glowing box.

JUDAS

Time's up.

Ray backs up and trips over a piece of furniture. He reaches under a chair cushion and pulls out the dagger.

RAMEN

Don't come near me! I'll kill you! Wait, I'm dreaming—–I'm asleep, right?

Crawling backward, Ray waves the dagger at him erratically.

The monster continues to approach slowly, one step at a time.

No! Leave me alone! Get away from me! Help!
(desperately)
HELP!!

He throws the dagger right toward the glowing box. The dagger strikes the box directly, and Judas drops it. He's startled enough that Ray regains composure.

Yeah, take that!

After a moment, RED LIGHT begins to fill the room. Ray's confidence slowly fades. SUDDENLY, the Alligator Man moves across the room supernaturally, and in an instant he's within inches of Ray . . .

FADE TO BLACK.

FINIS

END CREDITS

"Car" by Built to Spill plays, followed by "At the Helm" by Hieroglyphics, followed by "Heebie Jeebies" by Louis Armstrong.

Afterword

Hey Handsome

Me and my wife are in the middle of watching *Yellowstone*, the recent television series with Kevin Costner. We love it. But one of the things we find awkward is that nearly every character is extremely good looking, like supermodel level.

I pointed it out. I remember watching *The Last Action Hero* with Arnold Schwarzenegger when I was a kid, and a scene stuck with me. If my memory serves me, the boy in the movie (Danny Madigan) is trying to convince character Jack Slater that they are actors in a movie, and at one point he says something like: "Look around you, there are no unattractive people here!"

After reading my script, I got accused of that by my wife. She said it's obvious that everyone is labeled "handsome" or (like Sheila) "gorgeous." I'm not going to deny it, but I'll defend my reasoning because Ramen is writing a classic monster movie. While one of the story's themes is that Hollywood is no place for children, Ramen's (arguably innocent) movie script is about a possessed, murdering cannibal who dresses like an alligator and terrorizes a church parish. If my memory serves me correctly, all of the biggest horror movies (*A Nightmare on Elm Street, Halloween, Friday the 13th, Psycho*) feature half-naked, attractive men and women often getting undressed.

For example, people go skinny dipping, they take showers, they cheat on their partners, and they usually pay for it in a grim way. The horror movie *Scream* presented rules for a survivor in a horror movie, and one rule was that they can never have sex. The other two were: You cannot drink or do drugs; or say: "I'll be right back," or "Who's there?"

Two people die in this screenplay: Ramen (presumably), who's guilty of all three of *Scream's* rules and Randall, the dream representation of Ramen, who says "I'll be right back," to Sheila before his undoing, which isn't actually pictured.

Although that's a fun conversation to have when the topic is horror movies, a more in-depth discussion may be about what is touched on here when Ramen meets Professor Green that day at his office. Green tells Ramen that if you're going to have sex on screen, too much of it is boring. You have to balance it with violence.

You may laugh, but hopefully you take me seriously. That's what I intend. Smarter people than I have known for a very long time that people have something in their brains that make sex and violence attractive. And even though we do get bored (or worse) with seeing either of these things on their own for too long, when they are balanced well enough (sprinkled with wit and humor), sometimes you have, dare I say, a successful film.

Sex appeal may simply be a necessary part of the horror genre, a trope.

Hollywood Endings

The ending to *Dream of Writing* saw two variations before the one you read. The first was that Ramen turned down the money for his movie, and after his fight with Green his classmates hoisted him on their shoulders like in "Rudy," and carried him down the hallway and out into the sunset singing "For He's a Jolly Good Fellow." That ending was written in my 20s and stuck with me for over a decade.

When I re-envisioned the script at 40, I thought: "There is just no freaking way that this guy turns down a trilogy deal for over a million bucks." If he did, the hope is that he winds up with the right people in New Orleans and makes a great indie film for much less than Everest offers him (and maybe winds up with more dignity or at least say-so in its future). But in my experience that is almost, if not more, unlikely to happen. It does take money to make a movie! And if you're not swimming in it, it takes extreme courage bordering on idiocy to decide to go into tens of thousands of dollars of debt to make an indie movie with no guarantee that it will be successful or even watched by anyone. It did work, however, in the case of *Clerks.*

The second version is that Ramen sells the movie and stays in New Orleans with the love of his life, Jill, and they live happily ever after . . . until The Gator Man crosses over, kills Dave, and comes for them next (in a sequel). That works for me, but the entire script would have to be reworked—straightforward, where Ramen's dreaming is more predominant and causes problems for him and Jill that get sorted out eventually with his success.

In the end, neither of those endings substantially answered the bigger question of why Ramen's dreams are on a sacrificial altar. Although I could point to it: "Well, he's sacrificing himself to make this movie and yada yada," I didn't think it would be so apparent to an audience without explaining it. It was Ray on the altar the whole time, and in the final version, which you just read, I tried to state that as clearly as possible. Even though the ending is tough and tragic.

It's tragic, especially if you wanted to love Ramen along the way. I did. I felt like he was me at a certain point of telling this. But he was careless with Jill. He may have loved her, but he wanted to spend more time with his imaginary bombshell, didn't he? And that's who he really was. He wasn't really Ethan Hawke in *Before Sunset,* which inspired some of those long, romantic conversations between him and Jill. He was a young, obsessed, malcontented, greedy, alcoholic, drug-addict who traded in his life and friends for fame and fortune—what he really desired. He realized he made a mistake (maybe) but not before it was too late, and in a hallucinogenic state he (likely) committed suicide. I mean, unless you believe in talking alligators . . .

Homage Anyone

Maybe the most famous example of an enfant terrible, whom

I thought of much for Ray's character as a young filmmaker, is Harmony Korine. He made some shocking movies as a young man but has somehow survived the pitfalls of young stardom and power. I'm awfully glad he survived and still makes interesting movies. I dug around and read several articles about him and read most of the screenplay for *Jokes,* a film he never made but sold as a paperback, during my research phase. And I'd like to thank him for reminding me about the INT./EXT. signal for when writing about a scene in a moving car.

Next, the Coen brothers (*Fargo, The Big Lebowski*) inspired Producer #2, the oddball elderly lady in the Everest contract scene. She's cringey, but reminded me of a quirky Coen character. I also became inspired by their film *Blood Simple,* of which I read a partial screenplay during my research and borrowed the SUDDENLY– notation from. Side note: in the original draft, Ray wears a T-shirt in the first scene with John Turturro's face from the Coen's film *Barton Fink.* I didn't think it would resonate with most people like the film *E.T.,* which is one of my all-time favs.

The screenplay for *L.A. Confidential* by Brian Helgeland and Curtis Hanson was invaluable for me to become more comfortable with screenwriting. That script is something of perfection. I'm pretty sure I bought a used copy for pennies at Amoeba Records on Sunset Boulevard in Hollywood in 2013. I never even saw the movie, but . . . it's on my list.

Lastly, the music in this screenplay is something I'm proud to share here given the script has not been made into a movie, yet. Not sure if it's possible to show Dr. John on screen at this point, but he's intentionally walking down a dark alleyway so that with the right effects artist this could be achieved . . . Honestly, I think it would cost a fortune and therefore be unrealistic to have every song I mention on one soundtrack. A man can dream. I hope you found some meaning in the soundtrack as you went along.

Hoodoo Voodoo

I'll be the first to say that before this screenplay was written I knew not one iota about Haitian Voodoo or New Orleans Voodoo or African Voodoo, or any other Voodoo, ever. I didn't want to be that guy, either. You know, the one who misappropriates blatantly. So, I spent hours upon hours reading about potential Voodoo deities that could potentially possess Judas.

First, it was Papa Ghede (Baron Samedi), the top hat wearing, cigar smoking, voodoo St. Peter of the underworld. I figured it was a safe and well-traveled path of misappropriation for me to walk down, if nothing else. But I changed my mind.

I came up short beyond Samedi. Then, I read that there is human sacrifice in some outlaw sects of voodoo in the book *Secrets of Voodoo* by Milo Rigaud. The problem is that Milo Rigaud seems to have vanished at some point (and is likely deceased), and so I wonder about his writings. He states that the killer sects "prefer to wear blood-red [and] . . . are under the influence of Erzulie Zan-dor."

Guess what, there's no Wikipedia entry for Erzulie Zan-dor, but there is for "Ezili Dantor," and it is said that Haitians were under her influence when they drove the French colonists from Haiti in 1791. I suspect it's the same Erzulie. I also suspect that since writing is altogether scarce by Haitian Voodoo practitioners, most people who write about it are basing the spelling off of sound.

Further readings by Joan Dayan were illuminating, discussing Erzulie as a complex religious symbol, on one hand compared to the Blessed Mother and another something like Mother Nature—or something totally different, prayed to for fertility, wealth, strength, and revenge.

In the end, toward my best effort not to be a schmuck, I dropped the real deity for the "Evil Spirit of Obsession," as the thing that has both Judas and Ramen possessed.

Lastly, I hope that the amiable relationship between Jacques and Ramen is the most memorable thing about my use of voodoo in the story. The scene in the backyard ritual is inspired by an actual ca. 1950s photograph in my possession that is copyrighted, and I don't think I have permission to use it. Although, I wanted to use it as the cover for the paperback because it rocks.

The most positive thing I learned from studying more about

voodoo is that I may pray to my ancestors if I choose to, like my maw-maw, my granddad, or my cousin Mackie. That they are still with me at all times even at present like members of my immediate family.

Sequel

Although it's looking grim, Ray's got two more movies to write. Never know what's really going on with him . . .

About the Author

Gregory L. Fischer is a former Editor-In-Chief of the Gonzales *Weekly Citizen, The Donaldsonville Chief,* and the Plaquemine *Post-South* newspapers in Louisiana and contributor to *The Times-Picayune* in New Orleans. He is the author of *The Mayor of Mardi Gras: A Memoir.* He holds bachelor degrees in Creative Writing and Journalism from LSU. He attended graduate school for Professional Writing at Southeastern Louisiana University, where he served as Editor-In-Chief of the *Gambit* Creative Writing Journal for Students. He is certified in professional copy editing from New York University's School of Professional Studies and is the owner of Make It Write, a publishing services company in Baton Rouge, where he resides with his wife and stepchildren.